CARI
MORA

CARI
MORA

THOMAS HARRIS

WILLIAM HEINEMANN: LONDON

1 3 5 7 9 10 8 6 4 2

William Heinemann
20 Vauxhall Bridge Road
London SW1V 2SA

William Heinemann is part of the Penguin Random House group
of companies whose addresses can be found at
global.penguinrandomhouse.com.

Penguin
Random House
UK

First published in Great Britain by William Heinemann in 2019
First published in the United States by Grand Central Publishing in 2019

www.penguin.co.uk

A CIP catalogue record for this book is available from the British Library.

ISBN 9781785152207 (Hardback)
ISBN 9781785152191 (Trade Paperback)

Text design by Sean Ford

Printed and bound in Great Britain by Clays Ltd, Elcograf S.p.A.

Penguin Random House is committed to a sustainable future for our
business, our readers and our planet. This book is made from
Forest Stewardship Council® certified paper.

To Elizabeth Pace Barnes,
who gives me love and lends me
wisdom.

CHAPTER ONE

Two men talking in the middle of the night. They are 1,040 miles apart. One side of each face is lit by a cell phone. They are two half-faces talking in the dark.

"I can get the house where you say it is. Tell me the rest, Jesús."

The reply is faint through a crackle of static. "You paid one-fourth of what you promised." *Puff-puff.* "Send me the rest of the money. Send it to me." *Puff-puff.*

"Jesús, if I find what I want with no more help from you, you will receive nothing from me never."

"That is truer than you know. That's the truest thing you ever said in your life." *Puff-puff.* "What you want is sitting on fifteen kilos of Semtex…if you find it without my help you will be splattered on the moon."

"My arm is long, Jesús."

"It won't reach down from the moon, Hans-Pedro."

"My name is Hans-*Peter*, as you know."

"You'd put your hand on your peter if your arm was long enough? Is that what you said? I don't want your personal information. Quit wasting time. Send the money."

The connection is broken. Both men lie staring into the dark.

Hans-Peter Schneider is in a berth aboard his long black boat off Key Largo. He listens to a woman sobbing on the V-berth in the bow. He imitates her sobs. He is a good mimic. His own mother's voice comes out of his face, calling the crying woman's name. "Karla? Karla? Why are you crying, my dear child? It's just a dream."

Desperate in the dark, the woman is fooled for a second, then bitter wracking tears again.

The sound of a woman crying is Hans-Peter's music; it soothes him and he goes back to sleep.

In Barranquilla, Colombia, Jesús Villarreal lets the measured hiss of his respirator calm him. He breathes some oxygen from his mask. Through the common darkness he hears a patient out in the hospital ward, a man crying out to God for help, crying "Jesús!"

Jesús Villarreal whispers to the dark, "I hope God can hear you as well as I can, my friend. But I doubt it."

Jesús Villarreal calls information on his burner phone and obtains the number of a dance studio in Barranquilla. He pulls his oxygen mask aside to talk.

"No, I am not interested in learning to dance," he says into the telephone. "I am not dancing at this time. I want to speak to Don Ernesto. Yes you do know him. Say my name to him, he will know." *Puff-puff.*

CHAPTER TWO

Hans-Peter Schneider's boat slid very slowly past the great house on Biscayne Bay, water gurgling along the black hull.

Through his binoculars Hans-Peter watched Cari Mora, twenty-five, in her pajama pants and tank top as she stretched on the terrace in the early morning light.

"My goodness," he said. Hans-Peter's canine teeth are rather long and they have silver in them that shows when he smiles.

Hans-Peter is tall and pale, totally hairless. Lacking lashes, his eyelids touched the glass of his binoculars, making smudges. He wiped the eyepieces with a linen handkerchief.

The house-agent Felix stood behind him on the boat.

"That's her. The caretaker," Felix said. "She knows the house better than anybody, she can fix things. Learn the house from her and then I'll fire her smart ass before she can see anything she shouldn't see. She can save you some time."

"Time," Hans-Peter said. "Time. How much longer for the permit?"

"The guy renting the house now is shooting commercials. His permit is good for two more weeks."

"Felix, I want you to give me a key to that house." Hans-Peter speaks English with a German accent. "I want the key today."

"You go in there, something happens, you use my key, they know it's me. Like O.J.—you use my key, they know it's me." Felix laughed alone. "Listen, please, I will go to the renter today, ask him to let it go. You need to see the place in daylight, with people. You have to know it's a creepy son of a bitch in there. I went through four housekeepers before I got this one. She's the only one that's not afraid of it."

"Felix, you go to the renter. Offer him money. Up to ten thousand dollars. But right now you give me a key or you will be a floater in five minutes."

"You hurt the bitch, she can't help you," Felix said. "She sleeps there. She has to sleep there for the fire insurance. She works other places in the day sometimes. Wait and go in the day."

"I'm only going to look around. She'll never know I'm in the house."

Hans-Peter studied Cari through the glasses. She was on tiptoes filling a bird feeder now. It would be a waste to throw her away. With those interesting scars he could get a lot for her. Maybe $100,000— 35,433,184 Mauritanian ouguiya—from the Acroto Grotto Stump Club in Nouakchott. That's with all her limbs and no tattoos. If he had to customize her for top dollar, with the downtime, it would be more. A hundred and fifty thousand dollars. Chicken feed. There was between twenty-five and thirty million dollars in that house.

In the frangipani tree beside the terrace a catbird sang a song it had learned in the Colombian Cloud Forest and brought north to Miami Beach.

Cari Mora recognized the signature call of an Andean Solitaire that lived fifteen hundred miles away. The catbird sang with great enthusiasm. Cari smiled and paused to listen one more time to the song from her childhood. She whistled to the bird. It whistled back. She went inside the house.

On the boat Hans-Peter held out his hand for the key. Felix put the key on his palm without touching him.

"The doors are alarmed," Felix said. "But the sunroom door is faulted until we get some parts. It's the sunroom on the south side of the house. You got some lock picks? For the love of God scratch the tumblers before you use the key, and leave a pick on the steps in case something happens."

"I will do that for you, Felix."

"This is not a good idea," Felix said. "Fuck her up, you lose the knowledge."

At his car back at the marina, Felix took up the mat in the trunk to get to his burner phone stashed with the jack and tools. He dialed the number of a dance studio in Barranquilla, Colombia.

"No, señor," he said into the phone, whispering though he was outdoors. "I have delayed him with the permit as long as I can. He has his own lawyer for these things—he will find me out. He will just have the house. That's all. He knows no more than we do…Yes, I have the deposit. Thank you, señor, I will not fail you."

CHAPTER THREE

Cari Mora had a variety of day jobs. The one she liked was at the Pelican Harbor Seabird Station, where veterinarians and other volunteers rehabilitate birds and small animals. She maintained the treatment room and sterilized the instruments at the end of the workday. Sometimes with her cousin she catered the station's boat excursions.

Cari always went early for a chance to work with the animals. The station provided her with scrubs and she liked to wear them because they made her feel medical.

The veterinarians had learned to trust Cari, she was dexterous and careful with the birds, and today, with Dr. Blanco watching, she stitched the gular pouch beneath the beak of a white pelican injured by a fishhook. Pouch stitching is delicate work that must be done in layers, each stitched separately while the bird is anesthetized with gas.

It was peaceful, absorbing work. Very different from her childhood experience, closing soldiers' wounds in the field with a fast mattress stitch or a tourniquet or a poncho to cover a sucking chest wound, or pressing with her hand while she tore open a compress bandage with her teeth.

At the end of the day the pelican was sleeping it off in a recovery coop, and Dr. Blanco and the others had gone home.

Cari took an organic rat out of the freezer to thaw while she put the treatment room in order and refreshed the water in the outside flyways and pens.

When she had finished the room and sterilized the instruments, she opened a tamarind cola for herself and took the defrosted rat out to the wire-enclosed pens and flyways.

The great horned owl was on a perch in the high far corner of its flyway. She put the rat carcass through the wire onto a narrow shelf. She closed her eyes and tried to hear the owl coming before the wind from its great wings washed over her. The big bird never lit, but plucked up the food with one of its X-shaped feet and silently beat back up to its perch, where it opened its beak and throat startlingly wide and threw down the rat in one gulp.

The great horned owl was a permanent resident of

the Seabird Station. It could never be released as it had lost an eye in an accident with a power line and could not hunt, but it could fly very well. The owl was a popular visitor to the city schools for nature talks, where it put up with the close scrutiny of hundreds of schoolchildren, sometimes closing its one great eye and dozing during the lectures.

Cari sat on her overturned bucket with her back against the wire, under the scrutiny of the booby across the way recovering from a cut between its toes. Cari had closed the cut with a neat pulley stitch the vets had taught her.

In the nearby marina, the boats were lighting up and cozy couples were cooking in their galleys.

Caridad Mora, child of war, wanted to be a veterinarian. She had lived in the United States nine years on a shaky Temporary Protected Status, and her TPS could be canceled at any time by a governmental tantrum in the current sour atmosphere.

In the years before the immigration crackdown she had gotten a general equivalency high school diploma. She quietly added a home health aide license with the short six-week course plus her considerable life experience. But to go further in school she would have to show better papers than she had. The *migra*—ICE—was always watching.

In the short tropic twilight she took the bus back to the big house on the bay. It was almost dark when she got there, the palms already black against the last light.

She sat for a little while beside the water. The wind off the bay was full of ghosts tonight—young men and women and children who had lived or died in her arms as she tried to stanch their wounds, had fought to breathe and lived, or shivered out straight and gone limp.

Other nights the wind batted lightly at her like the memory of a kiss, of eyelashes brushing her face, sweet breath on her neck.

Sometimes this, sometimes that, but always the wind was full.

Cari sat outside listening to the frogs, the many-eyed lotus in the pond watching her. She watched the entrance hole of an owl house she had made out of a wooden crate. No face appeared yet. Tree frogs were peeping.

She whistled the song of the Andean Solitaire. No bird replied. She felt a little empty as she went inside in the hard time of day when you eat alone.

Pablo Escobar had owned this house, but he never lived here. Those who knew him thought he bought it for family to use if he was ever extradited to the United States.

The house had been in and out of the legal system since Escobar's death. A series of playboys and fools and real estate speculators had owned it over the years—plungers who bought it from the courts and held on to it for a little while as their fortunes went up and down. The house was still full of their follies: movie props, monster mannequins, everything lunging and reaching. There were fashion mannequins, lobby cards, jukeboxes, horror-film props, some sex furniture. In the living room was an early electric chair from Sing Sing that had only killed three, its amperage last adjusted by Thomas Edison.

A progression of lights on and off up through the house as Cari made her way through the mannequins, the crouching movie monsters, the seventeen-foot Mother Alien from the Planet Zorn to reach her bedroom at the top of the stairs. A last light in her bedroom winked out.

CHAPTER FOUR

With Felix's key in hand, Hans-Peter Schneider could creep the house in Miami Beach as
he was dying to do. He could creep it with the girl
Cari Mora asleep in her hotness upstairs.

Hans-Peter was in his living quarters in an un-
marked warehouse on Biscayne Bay near the old
Thunderboat Alley in North Miami Beach, his black
boat tied up in the adjacent boathouse. He sat naked
on a stool in the center of his tiled shower room, letting the many nozzles on the walls beat water on him
from all directions. He was singing in his German
accent: "…just singing in the rains. What a glorious
feeling, I am haaaappy again."

He could see his reflection in the glass side of his
liquid cremation machine where he was dissolving
Karla, a girl who hadn't worked out for business.

In the rising mist Hans-Peter's image on the glass looked like a daguerreotype. He struck the pose of Rodin's *The Thinker* and watched himself out of the corner of his eye. A faint smell of lye rose with the steam.

Interesting to see himself as *The Thinker* reflected on the glass, while behind the glass, in the tank, Karla's bones were beginning to stand up out of the paste the corrosive lye water had made of the rest of her. The machine rocked, sloshing fluid back and forth. The machine burped and bubbles came up.

Hans-Peter was very proud of his liquid cremation machine. He'd had to pay a premium for it, as liquid cremation was becoming all the rage with ecology enthusiasts eager to avoid the carbon footprint of cremation by fire. The liquid method left no carbon footprint, or print of any kind. If a girl did not work out, Hans-Peter could just pour her down the loo in liquid form—and with no harmful effect on the groundwater. His little work song was:

"Call Hans-Peter—that's the name!—and away go troubles down the drain—Hans-Peter!"

Karla had not been a total loss—she had provided Hans-Peter with some amusement and he was able to sell both her kidneys.

Hans-Peter could feel the pleasant heat from his cremation machine radiate across the shower room, though he kept the temperature of the lye water at only 160 degrees Fahrenheit to prolong the process. He enjoyed watching Karla's skeleton emerge slowly from her flesh, and, like a reptile, he was drawn to warmth.

He was deciding what to wear to creep the house. His white latex plugsuit was newly stolen from a fantasy convention and he was mad for it, but it squeaked when his thighs rubbed together. No. Something black and comfortable with no Velcro to rasp if he decided to take off his clothes in the house while he looked at Cari Mora asleep. And a change of clothes in a plastic bag in case he got wet or sticky, and an ornate flask of bleach to destroy DNA, should it come to that. And his stud finder.

He sang a song in German, a folk song Bach used in the Goldberg Variations called "Sauerkraut and Beets Are Driving Me Away."

It was nice to be excited. To be going on a creep. To be getting back at Pablo in his infernal sleep...

Hans-Peter Schneider was in the hedge beside the big house at 1 a.m. There was a lot of moon, palm shadows black as blood lay on the moonlit ground. When wind moves the big fronds a shadow on the ground can look like the shadow of a man. Sometimes it is the shadow of a man. Hans-Peter waited for a puff of wind and moved with the shadows across the lawn.

The house still radiated the heat of the day. It felt like a big warm animal as he stood close against the wall. Hans-Peter pressed himself against the side of the house and felt the heat up and down his body. He could feel the moonlight, itchy on his head. He thought of a newborn kangaroo working its way up its mother's belly toward the warm pouch.

The house was dark. He could see nothing through the tinted glass of the sunroom. Some of the metal hurricane shutters were down. Hans-Peter stuck a pick into the lock and raked the tumblers twice to scratch them.

He pushed Felix's key slowly into the lock. He had the good freezing feeling. It was so intimate for Hans-Peter, pressing against the warm house and pushing the key into the lock. He could hear the tumblers engage in a tiny series of clicks, like the insects talking when he revisited a woman dead for days in the bush and warmed wonderfully—warmed warmer than life by the larval mounds.

The oval bow of the key was flush now against the rose of the lock. Flush as he would be against her if he decided to go upstairs. Stay stuck to her until she got too cool. Sadly, she would cool faster than the house does as it sheds the heat of the sun. In the air-conditioning she wouldn't stay warm for long even if he pulled the covers up over them and snuggled. They never did stay warm. So soon clammy, so soon cool.

He didn't need to decide now. He might just follow his heart. It was fun to see if he could keep from following his heart. Heart HEAD, head HEART, bump. He hoped she smelled good. *Sauerkraut and beets are driving me away.*

He turned the knob and the weather-stripping hissed as he pushed the door open. The stud finder taped to the toe of his shoe would detect any metallic alarm mat hidden under a carpet. He slid his foot across the sunroom floor before he put his weight on it. Then he stepped inside, into the cool darkness, away from the shadows moving on the lawn and the heat of the moon on his skull.

A twang and rustle in the corner behind him.

"What the fuck, Carmen?" a bird said.

Hans-Peter's pistol was in his hand and he had no memory of drawing it. He stood still. The bird rustled again in its cage, shuffled up and down the perch and muttered.

Silhouettes of mannequins against the moonlit windows. Did any of them move? Hans-Peter moved among them in the dark. An extended plaster hand touched him as he passed.

It is here. It is here. The gold is here. Es ist hier! He knew it. If the gold had ears it could hear him if he called to it from this spot where he stood in a parlor. Draped furniture, a draped piano. He went into the bar with its pool table draped to the floor with sheets. The icemaker dumped a tumble of ice and he went into a crouch, waiting, listening, thinking.

The girl had a lot of information about the house. He should harvest that information before anything else. He could always get the money for her later. She wouldn't be worth more than a few thousand dead, and to get even that he'd have to ship her in dry ice.

It made no sense to disturb her, but she was so fetching, so heartwarming on the terrace and he wanted to look at her asleep. He was entitled to some fun. Maybe he could just drip a little on the bed-clothes, on her scarred arms, nothing more. Oh, a drop or two on her sleeping cheek, little facial, what the hell? A little might run into the corner of her eye. Hello. Prime her eye for the tears to come.

The telephone in his pocket buzzed against his thigh. He moved it around until it felt good. He looked at the text from Felix and that felt even better. The text said:

I got it. I got him to give up his permit for 10K and some good shit to come. Our permit clear tomorrow. Can move in now!

Hans-Peter reclined on the carpet underneath the draped pool table and punched out some texts with what he called his zinc finger. The nail of his forefinger was distorted by the same genetic affliction that made him hairless. He had learned about zinc finger before he was expelled from medical school on moral grounds. Fortunately his father had been too old to beat him hard for the failure. The nail was sharp and useful for clearing his hairless nasal passages, so susceptible to mold and spores and the pollens of spiny amaranth and rape.

Cari Mora came awake in the dark and did not know why. Her waking reflex was to listen for the warning sounds of the forest. She came to herself then, and without moving her head she looked around the big bedroom. All the tiny lights were glowing—TV cable box, the thermostat, the clock—but the alarm-pad light was green instead of red.

A single beep had awakened her when someone turned off the alarm downstairs. Now the alarm light blinked as something passed a motion sensor in the foyer on the floor below.

Cari Mora pulled on some sweats and got her baseball bat from under the bed. Her phone and her knife and her bear repellent spray were in her pockets. She went out into the hall and called down the winding stairs.

"Who is it? You better say something now."

Nothing for fifteen seconds. Then a voice from below said "Felix."

Cari rolled her eyes up at the ceiling and hissed between her teeth.

She turned on the lights and went down the spiral staircase. She took the bat with her.

Felix stood at the bottom of the stairs, beneath a movie figure, the toothy space raptor from the Planet Zorn.

Felix did not look like he was drunk. He did not have a weapon in his hands. He had his hat on in the house.

Cari stopped four steps from the bottom. She did not feel his piggy eyes on her. Good, that.

"You call me before you come here in the night," she said.

"I got a renter, last minute," Felix said. "Movie people. They pay good. They want you to stay because you know the place, maybe cook too, I don't know yet. I got you the job with them. You should thank me. You should give me something when they pay you big movie money."

"What kind of a movie?"

"I don't know. I don't care."

"You bringing this news at five in the morning?"

"If they're willing to pay, they get their way," Felix said. "They want to be inside before daylight."

"Felix, look here at me. If it's porn you know what I say to that. I'm walking if it's that."

A lot of pornographic movie production was moving to Miami after the passage of Los Angeles County's Measure B, requiring the use of condoms onscreen, stifling freedom of expression.

She'd had trouble with Felix about this before.

"It's not dirty movies. It's like, reality something. They want two-hundred-twenty-volt hookups and fire extinguishers. You know where all that stuff's at, right?" He took out of his jacket a wrinkled City of Miami Beach filming permit and told her to get him some tape.

In fifteen minutes she heard a boat close inshore on Biscayne Bay.

"Leave the dock lights off," Felix said.

Hans-Peter Schneider is extremely clean much of the time in his public life and smells good to casual acquaintances. But when Cari shook his hand in the kitchen, she caught a whiff of brimstone off him. Like the smell of a burning village with dead inside the houses.

Hans-Peter noted her good hard palm, and smiled his wolfish smile. "Shall we speak English or Spanish?"

"As you wish."

Monsters know when they are recognized, just as bores do. Hans-Peter was accustomed to reactions of distaste and fear as his behavior revealed him. On exquisite occasions, the reaction was an agonized pleading for a quicker death. Some people beeped to him quicker than others.

Cari just looked at Hans-Peter. She did not blink. The black pupils of her eyes had the smudge of intelligence.

Hans-Peter tried to see his reflection in her eyes but disappointingly he could not see himself. *What a looker! And I don't think she knows it.*

A moment of reverie as he made up a little couplet. *I cannot see my reflection in the black pools of your eyes / You will be hard to break but, broken, what a prize!* He'd do it in German too, with a tune, when he had time. Use "hörig" for "broken," more like "enslaved." Use the tune from "Sauerkraut and Beets." Sing it in the shower. Maybe to her, if she happened to be recuperating, begging to be clean.

At the moment, he needed her goodwill. Showtime now.

"You have worked here a long time," he said. "Felix tells me you are a good worker, you know the house well."

"I've watched the house five years on and off. I helped with some repairs."

"Does the pool house leak?"

"No, it's good. You can cool it if you want to. The pool house A/C is on a separate box with a circuit breaker on the garden wall."

From the corner Hans-Peter's man Bobby Joe was

staring at Cari. Even in cultures where staring is not rude, Bobby Joe's stare would be rude. His eyes were orange-yellow, like those of certain turtles. Hans-Peter beckoned to him.

Bobby Joe stood too close to Cari when he came.

She could read the tattoo *"Balls and All!"* in cursive on the side of his neck under his grown-out jail haircut. His fingers were lettered LOVE and HATE. MANUELA was written in his palm. The end of the strap on the back of his cap stuck far out to the side owing to the smallness of his skull. A memory of something bad pierced her and was gone.

"Bobby Joe, put the heavy stuff in the pool house for now," Hans-Peter said.

When Bobby Joe passed behind Cari, his knuckles brushed her buttocks. She touched the inverted cross of St. Peter that hung from her neck on a bead chain.

"Is the electric current and water turned on all over the house?" Hans-Peter said.

"Yes," Cari said.

"Do you have two-hundred-twenty-volt current?"

"Yes. In the laundry and behind the kitchen stove. There's a golf cart charger in the garage with a two-twenty outlet and two long extension cords on hooks above it. Use the red one, not the black. Somebody cut the ground prong off the black one. It's got two twenty-amp circuit breakers beside it. In the pool house it's all GFIs."

"Do you have the floor plan?"

"There are architect's drawings and an electrician's diagram in the library, in the floor-level cabinet."

"Is the alarm connected to a central office, or the police?"

"No, it's manual only with a siren on the street. Four zones, doors and motions."

"Is there food in the house?"

"No. You are eating here?"

"Yes. Some of us."

"Sleeping here?"

"Until our job is finished. Some of us will sleep and eat here too."

"There are the lunch trucks. They work construction jobs up and down the street. They're pretty good. Better early in the week. You will hear the horn. I like Comidas Distinguidas the best, and the Salazar Brothers are good. The last film crew used them. They have 'Hot Eats' on the side of the truck. I have a phone number for them if you want them to cater."

"I want you to cater," Hans-Peter said. "You could get food and cook one good meal a day? You don't have to serve the table, just make the food like buffet. I will pay good."

Cari needed the money. She was fiercely fast and

thorough in the kitchen, as women are who come up hard in Miami working in rich people's houses.

"I can do that. I'll fix the meal."

Cari had worked with construction crews. In her teens when she cooked from midnight on and served food from the lunch trucks in cutoff jeans, the carpenters swarmed and business went way up. In Cari's experience the majority of the men in the hard physical trades are well-intentioned, courteous even. They are just hungry for everything.

But Cari could see Hans-Peter's crew of three and she did not like the look of them. Jailbirds with jail tattoos made with match-soot ink and an electric toothbrush. They were carrying a heavy magnetic drill press and two jackhammers into the pool house along with a single movie camera.

Women working in the trades can tell you the rule of thumb with a rough crew in a secluded place—it was true in the jungle and it was true here—bigger is safer. Most of the time if there are more than two men in the crew, civilization prevails; they won't start something with a woman unless they are drunk. This was a rougher crew than that. They stared at Cari when she led Hans-Peter to the electrical boxes mounted in the narrow corridor between the high hedge and the boundary wall of the property. She could feel them thinking *Pull a train, pull a train*. More than their oafish stares, she was aware of Hans-Peter walking behind her.

Behind the hedge Hans faced her. Full-face and smiling, he resembled a white stoat. "Felix said he went through four housekeepers before he found you. The others were afraid of this place, all the creepy stuff. But it doesn't frighten you? I would be interested to know why."

Do not engage him, do not answer, her instinct told her.

Cari shrugged. "You'll need to pay for the groceries in advance."

"I'll reimburse," he said.

"I'll need the cash up front. Seriously."

"You are a serious person. You sound like a Colombian—so pretty the Spanish. How did you get to stay in the U.S., did you try to use 'credible fear'? Did immigration allow you credible fear?"

"I think two hundred and fifty dollars will cover the groceries for now," Cari said.

"Credible fear," Hans-Peter said. He was enjoying the planes of her face, thinking how pain might affect them. "The things in the house, the horror movie props, do not scare you, Cari. And why is that? You see they are only the imaginings of mall rats to scare other mall rats, don't you? You see that, don't you, Cari? You know the difference. You are closer to the verities—do you know verities? Las verdades, la realidad? How did you learn the difference? Where did you see something truly fearful?"

"Good chuletas are on sale at Publix, and I should pick up some fuses," Cari said, and left him standing under the spiderwebs behind the hedge.

"Chuletas are on sale at Publix," Hans said to himself in Cari's voice. He has a startling ability to mimic.

Cari took Felix aside. "Felix, I am not staying here overnight."

"The fire insurance—" he began.

"Then stay here yourself. Best you sleep on your back. I'll do the meal."

"Cari, I'm telling you—"

"And I'm telling you. If I stay something stupid will happen. You will not like what happens next and neither will they."

CHAPTER FIVE

"Don Ernesto wants to know what's going on at Pablo's old house," Captain Marco said. "When can we see?"

Marco sat with two other men under an open shed in the boatyard in the early evening. A breeze stirred the flags on the freighters tied up along the Miami River. Captain Marco's boat squeaked against a dock piled with crab traps.

"I can go in with the gardeners at seven in the morning if Claudio's truck will start," Benito said. "By contract they have to let us in every two weeks to drag off the limbs and cut the weeds." Benito was old and leathery. His eyes were bright. With his banana fingers he rolled a perfect cigarette of Bugler tobacco, twisted the end and lit it with a kitchen match, which he struck with his thumbnail.

"Jesús Villarreal claims the gold is there at the house," Captain Marco said. "He brought it up for Pablo in his boat in '89. Don Ernesto says the film crew at the house now is fake, they're digging under the house."

"Jesús was a good man in a boat," Benito said. "I thought he was dead with Pablo. I thought we were all dead except me, such as I am."

"You are way too wicked to die," Antonio said, and poured the old man a drink from the bottle on the table. Antonio was twenty-seven, fit in his pool service T-shirt.

The three men under the shed kept a casual eye on Miami for their mentor in Cartagena, as a sideline. They all had the same tattoo, in various places. The tattoo was a bell hanging on a fishhook.

Music drifted over the water from a restaurant downriver, under the Miami skyline.

"Who's digging under the house?" Antonio said.

"Hans-Peter Schneider and his crew," Marco said.

"I have seen Hans-Peter Schneider," Benito said. "Have you ever seen him? You first see him, you are sad he could be ill. When you know him he looks like a dick wearing glasses."

"He's from Paraguay," Marco said. "They say he is a very bad man."

"He believes so himself," Benito said, putting the tobacco tin back in the bib of his overalls. "I saw him shoot a man across the ass for loafing when he was digging up Pablo's house outside Bogotá looking for the money. He is crazy in a bad way."

"Hans-Peter Schneider has business here," Antonio said. "He's back and forth—he's got a couple of whorehouses in Miami, the Roach Motel and the other one out by the airport, and a video peep. His high point, he had two real kinky bars—The Low Gravy and one called Congress. The Health Department found out they were serving English breakfasts upstairs and the county pulled his liquor license. ICE tried to bounce him once for trafficking girls and boys. Now he's got nothing with his name on it. It's like he doesn't exist anymore. But he's in and out, and he collects the money."

Antonio fished often with the young policemen and he knew things.

He tossed back the last of his drink. "I can service the pool after eight tomorrow. It leaks and I can drag out fixing it."

"What about the foreman, the agent for the house, is it still Felix?" Captain Marco said.

Benito nodded. "Felix is a shit crayon. His work hat cost five hundred fifty dollars plus tax, what does that tell you? The good thing is he doesn't notice much. The young lady in the house is very nice, though. Wonderfully nice."

"You can say that again," Antonio said.

"She should not stay there with Hans-Peter Schneider."

"I spoke with her on the phone, she's not staying at night," Antonio said.

"Too bad Schneider has seen her at all," Benito said.

"Go in tomorrow," Captain Marco said. "I'll bring the boat up the bay about nine o'clock with my crew and work the crab traps. We'll foul a line and hang out there for a while. If there's a problem, Benito, take off your hat and fan yourself with it. We'll come in for you. If you have your hands up, knock your hat off your head by accident. We'll come in hot if we have to—when you hear the motor get low. Don't be Marines, Don Ernesto just wants to know what's going on at the house."

Thunderheads stood over the Everglades to the west. Lightning pulsed inside them. To the east the skyline of Miami glittered like an iceberg.

Beside the crab boat at the dock a manatee surfaced to breathe and wheeze. The manatee listened for the soft breath of the calf beside her. Satisfied, she sank out of sight.

CHAPTER SIX

Benito came early with the contract gardeners to the big house on Biscayne Bay. He was chopping weeds against the seawall at midmorning when he heard the tour boat coming. The old man shot a look at the second-floor terrace. The thug Umberto in his black muscle shirt had heard the boat coming too. He was dragging a dusty movie camera out onto the terrace.

Benito could see the suppressor on Umberto's AR-15 sticking two inches above the railing. The old gardener shook his head. *The carelessness of young people. No, that's an old-man thought. It is not Umberto's youth that is to blame, it is his stupidity, which he will not outgrow.*

"Take the reflector with you," Felix shouted to Umberto from his seat indoors in the air-conditioning. Felix in his $550-plus-tax Panama hat, actually made in Ecuador.

Biscayne Bay lay gray-green under the overcast sky, and beyond the bay stood the towers of downtown Miami, four miles across the water from this house on Miami Beach.

The tour boat was still three houses down, close inshore, coming down Millionaire's Row on the high tide. It was a big pontoon boat with a surrey top, a pop tune playing on its speakers. The guide had been a carnival barker in his time. His amplified voice bounced off the big houses on the waterfront, many of them shuttered for the summer.

"On our left, the home of music mogul Greenie Pardee. Look carefully and you can see the sun reflect off an entire wall of gold records that adorns his den."

The tour boat was almost even with Benito now. He could see the pale faces of the tourists along the railing.

The guide keyed music from the movie *Scarface* and talked over it:

"On a darker note, to our left, where you see the tattered green awnings, the faded wind sock, the overgrown helicopter pad—that is the house once owned by Pablo Escobar, dope kingpin, murderer, bloody billionaire, slain by police on a rooftop in Colombia.

"Nobody lives there now. The house is rented out for filming until a new owner comes along. Say! We're in luck! Looks like they're shooting a movie today! Can anybody spot a star?"

The guide waved to Benito. Benito raised his hand, a solemn wave. The tourists saw that the old man was not a star. Few of them waved back.

Farther out on the flat green water Captain Marco's crab boat worked a trapline, its diesel drowning out the guide from time to time.

Up on the terrace Umberto unscrewed a wing nut on the camera, then screwed it back tight.

"Take the lens cap off," Felix said from his cool seat indoors. "Be convincing." Felix with the two-hundred-dollar shades.

"You can buy the Escobar house if you want it," the guide said as the boat slid past. "All you need is twenty-seven million dollars. Now, four houses down we're coming to the palatial home of leading pornographer Leslie Mullens. Does *Around the World in Eighty Ways* ring a bell? And ironically his next-door neighbor is Alton Fleet, televangelist and faith healer, whose ministry numbers millions of followers across the land, spellbound by his faith healing services broadcast from Cathedral of the Palms." The boat moved on, the tinny voice trailing away.

A jackhammer in the basement shivered the Escobar house. Dust rose from the terrace. Lizards ran for the cracks.

Old Benito hoped Cari Mora would come outside. It would be very pleasant to see her and to look at her and hear her voice.

Bubbles in the swimming pool indicated that Antonio, in his scuba gear, was still submerged looking for the leak. His presence encouraged Benito to think that Cari might come out. And in a few minutes, sure enough, here she came wearing baggy hospital scrubs.

Caridad Mora carried two frosted glasses of mint tea, and—oh YES!—she was bringing one to Benito. He could smell her excellent aroma and he could smell the mint in the tea. He lifted his hat. He could smell his hat too, so he put it back on quickly.

"Hola, Señor Benito," she said.

"Mil gracias, Señorita Cari. You are a pleasant sight today and always." *It is easy to see why Cari's cousin won the beauty title of Miss Hawaiian Tropic at no less a venue than the Nikki Beach club,* Benito thought. *Cari could have entered too and won easily if it were not for the scars on her arms. Truly they are only snaky lines on her clear brown-gold skin. The scars are more exotic than disfiguring. Like cave paintings of wavy snakes. Experience decorates us.*

Cari smiled at him; Benito felt that she saw him for the man he was. She left him a little breathless, like a shot of overproof rum, like a puff of Two-Toke Sour Diesel. Like his Lupe did forty years ago.

Benito looked into her face. "Cari?"

"Yes, mi señor?"

"You must be very careful with these people."

She looked straight back at him. "I know. Thank you, Señor Benito."

Cari stopped by the swimming pool and considered the trail of bubbles. She slipped off her shoe and put her foot on the head of the submerged Antonio. He came up sputtering more than he strictly needed to. Antonio in his wet pool service T-shirt, a black Gothic cross earring in his left ear.

Cari put his glass of tea on the tiles beside the pool.

Antonio pushed up his mask and grinned at her.

"Gracias, Guapa!! Hey, I need to talk to you! Guess what? I got tickets to Juanes at the Hard Rock! Great seats! Any closer and he'd fall off the stage looking at you. Dinner and the show, how about it?"

She was shaking her head before he even finished.

"No, Antonio. Plenty of girls would love to go with you. I can't."

"Why not?"

"Because you have a wife is why."

"Baby, it's not like that. It's just a green card thing. We don't even—"

"A wife is a wife, Antonio. Thank you, but no."

She walked back toward the house under Antonio's avid gaze.

"Gracias for the tea, Guapa," he said.

"Exhibit manners, Antonio," Benito called from a distance. He was smiling. "Princesa Guapa to you!"

"Discúlpeme! Gracias, Princesa Guapa!" Antonio called after her.

She laughed but did not look back at him.

Benito took a deep drink, set his tea on the seawall. *That was very refreshing. The tea is good too.*

Behind him in the center of the swimming pool stood a plaster copy of the *Winged Victory of Samothrace*, headless, her wings spread. A previous owner had believed he was buying it from the Louvre.

Benito looked at the *Victory*, thinking. *I wonder if she lost her dream of flight along with her head, or if I can still see it there in the heat shimmer above the stump of her neck, or maybe it is still in her heart, where we keep dreams. Perhaps that is an old-man thought I should avoid. I wonder if Cari can still keep dreams in her heart after the things she has seen. I have seen things too. I hope the ceiling of her heart is higher than the ceiling of mine.*

At midafternoon an Uber brought Cari Mora into the driveway with a lot of groceries. The driver helped her unload a trunkful of bags and set them on the lawn. Quickly Benito put down his hoe and picked up the four bags that looked heaviest.

"Thank you, Señor Benito," she said. Together they went through the side door of the house, into a sunroom with a big cockatoo in a cage. To get attention, the bird had hung upside down from its perch and lifted the edge of the newspaper cage liner with its beak to spill seed and seed hulls onto the floor.

Benito and Cari carried the groceries into the kitchen. It was noisy in the kitchen, noise coming up from below, where power tools were working. A red extension cord snaked from the laundry room through a door to the basement and down the stairs. Another cord was plugged in behind the stove. Benito wanted to see into the basement. Some acetylene tanks were standing against the wall of the kitchen, waiting to be carried down. He put down the four bags of groceries on the counter and had started for the open door to look into the basement when Umberto came up the stairs into the kitchen.

"What the fuck are you doing in here?" he said.

"I am bringing in groceries," Benito said.

"Get the fuck out. Nobody is allowed in the house." To Cari: "We told you that. Nobody in the house."

"I am bringing in groceries," Benito said. "And not flushing a dirty mouth in front of a lady. You could bring the groceries in, if you can lift them."

It was not a smart thing to say. Sometimes old men don't care how foolish something is if it feels good right away. Benito had his hand inside the bib of his overalls.

Umberto could not be sure what Benito might have in there behind the bib. In fact, Benito had, just beneath his sternum, a 1911A1 Colt .45 pistol converted to a .460 Rowland, gift of his doting nephew, who blew up watermelons with it on the range. Benito carried it cocked and locked.

Umberto thought the old man looked a little crazy in the face.

"No one is allowed in the house," Umberto said. "She could get fired for letting you in. Want me to tell the boss?"

Cari turned to Benito. "Thank you, mi señor," she said. "It's all right. Please, I can manage the rest."

"Excuse you," Benito said into Umberto's face and left the kitchen.

A big school of crevalle jacks surged by in the late afternoon with a roar like a train, chasing mullet along the seawall where Benito cut weeds with his hoe. Benito could smell them and he leaned over the waist-high seawall to watch as the powerful fish raced by, their forked tails flashing and small fish and pieces of fish flying in the air, an oily urine smell rising from the water behind them. *Like us*, Benito thought. *Kill and gobble like us.*

Through the soles of his shoes he could feel the jackhammer working in the basement of the house.

Then the trembling ground against the seawall gave way beneath his hoe, dirt falling to splash far below. He was looking down into a new hole in the lawn against the seawall. The hole was the size of his hat. Many feet underneath the lawn he could see the light glint off black water, swelling and falling away down there in the dark underground, inside the seawall. He stepped back onto the concrete edge of the patio. He could hear the water gurgling under there, sucking in and out under the seawall. The hole breathed with the swells, exhaling the stench of rotting meat.

Benito looked up at the high terrace. Felix was up there haranguing Umberto with his back to the garden. Benito snaked a cell phone out of his overalls and turned on the flash. He went to his knees beside the hole. Dexterous for such an old man, he put his hand down in the hole and took two flash pictures of the space he could not see, turning his face from the smell.

Felix was still talking up on the balcony.

Benito hissed at Antonio, standing in the pool. Antonio put down his tea fast and came out of the water. He went with Benito behind the pool house where spare flagstones and roof tiles were stacked.

"Let's take a flagstone, we'll put it over the hole and you go back to work," Benito said.

"You calling Marco?" Antonio said. He looked

out over the bay to the crab boat. The crew had opened a barrel of bait and the gulls and a pelican were following the boat.

Benito and Antonio carried a flagstone and covered the hole.

"Stay on the patio, don't step off on the grass, it could cave some more," Benito said. "You should get back in the pool now."

The old gardener got a potted plant and put it on top of the flagstone. He was raking dirt around it when he heard Felix behind him.

"The hell are you doing?" Felix said.

"Covering up a sinkhole. We'll bring some dirt and—"

"Let me see. Open it up."

The hole was webbed with roots.

"Shit," Felix said. He took out his cell phone. "Get me a cushion out of the pool house. Hurry up."

Kneeling on the cushion to preserve his linen trousers, Felix held his telephone down in the hole and took a picture using his flash.

"Cover it up and put the plant on it," he said.

"Like it was before?" Benito said.

Felix put his phone back in his pants and took from his pocket another expensive accessory, an ornate out-the-front spring dagger for which he had paid $400. He popped the blade out and cleaned a fingernail. He held up the knife and, looking at Benito, slid the blade back into the handle. With the other hand he extended a folded hundred-dollar bill. "Silencio sobre esto, Viejo. Me entiendes?"

Benito looked him in the face. He waited a beat before he took the money and crushed it in his hand. "Claro, señor."

"Go in the front-yard garden, help them up there."

Antonio was taking some tracer dye out of his pack beside the pool when Felix told him, "Pack up your shit, you're finished for the day."

"I haven't found the leak yet."

"Pack your stuff and get out. I'll call when I want you to come back."

Antonio waited until Felix turned away before he took off his swim fins. On the bottom of his foot was the tattoo, a bell suspended from a fishhook, along with his blood type. Quickly he slipped on his shoes.

Inside the house, Cari let the big white cockatoo out of its cage. It was standing on her wrist eyeing her earrings when the doorbell rang. She went past draped furniture and a jukebox to the side entrance, still carrying the bird. Antonio was waiting at the door. He looked around quickly.

"Listen, Cari. You need to be away from here. Stay inside right now. Don't see nothing. Be dumb until they send you away—are you listening to me? If they don't fire you by the end of the day, take the bird home with you. Say the dust is hurting it. Get the flu at home and don't come back."

"Touch it, Mamacita!" the bird said.

Felix came around the side of the house in a hurry. "I told you to get your ass out of here, now move it."

Antonio fronted him up. "You kiss your mother with that mouth?"

"Get out," Felix said as he stalked away, fumbling with his cell phone.

Antonio's pool service truck was parked by the gardening crew's van. Three of the gardeners were stacking fallen palm fronds, a fourth was running a weed eater in the long driveway. When Antonio threw the last of his equipment in the back of the truck he saw Cari standing in the front door of the house. She was still holding the bird. She smiled at him and waved goodbye.

Behind the house Felix punched a number into his phone.

CHAPTER SEVEN

Hans-Peter Schneider and Bobby Joe of the yellow eyes arrived in Bobby Joe's truck to find the driveway of the Escobar house blocked by the gardener's van. Bobby Joe drove Hans-Peter across the lawn and the flower beds to the front door.

Bobby Joe's truck had a lift kit, a simulated roll bar of chromed plastic and a pair of TruckNutz rubber testicles hanging from the trailer hitch. His bumper sticker said IF I'D KNOWN THIS I WOULD OF PICKED MY OWN COTTON.

Felix was there to greet them. He whipped off his hat.

"Patrón," Felix said.

"Who found it?" Schneider was already walking toward the waterside garden. He wore linen in the heat, and black patent huaraches to match his watch-band.

"The old man who cuts the weeds." Felix indicated Benito, loading tools into the van with the other gardeners. "He doesn't know anything, I took care of him."

Hans-Peter watched Benito for a minute. "Show me the hole," he said.

At the hole against the seawall, Felix and Bobby Joe dragged the flagstone aside. Hans-Peter stepped back, waving the air in front of his face.

Felix showed Hans-Peter the picture he'd taken holding his camera down in the hole. He had moved the picture to an iPad.

The sea had come under the seawall to eat out a cave beneath the concrete patio extending almost to the house. The roots of trees hung down into the cave like crooked chandeliers. Pilings knobbed with barnacles supported the patio above. The water level at this stage of the tide left about four feet of space between the water and the ceiling. The erosion had exposed under the patio half of a sunken iron gravel barge, part of the landfill and dredging that built Miami Beach.

At the far end of the black cave, barely lit by the flash, the bottom shelved up into a beach. A shiny cube larger than a refrigerator stood at the far end of the cave, almost flush against the foundation of the house. Felix spread his fingers on the iPad, enlarging the picture. Beside the cube, at water's edge, were a human skull and the back half of a dog.

"All the time we're digging in the basement and the sea was digging for us," Hans-Peter Schneider said. "Gott mit uns! It could hold a ton of gold. Who knows about it?"

"Nobody, señor. The other gardeners were in the front yard. The old man is an ignorant bracero."

"Maybe it is you who is ignorant—or is it whom is ignorant? I can never remember English grammar. I've seen that old fart before. Get him. Send the rest of the gardeners home. Tell the old one we need him to help us. Say we'll give him a ride."

Out on the bay the loud crab boat was working back up the trapline, dumping rebaited traps now, the two deckhands throwing a trap overboard about every twenty yards in a steady rhythm.

In the wheelhouse Captain Marco fixed his binoculars on the garden of the Escobar house. He saw Hans-Peter and the others in the waterside garden, and he saw Felix and Bobby Joe bring Benito to join them.

"Rodrigo, drop the trapline," Captain Marco said. He pointed with his chin. "Mayday, muchachos. Strap up. We go in hot if Benito has to jump."

On the patio, Benito stood in front of Hans-Peter.

"I know you," Hans-Peter said.

"Old men look pretty much alike, señor. I do not remember you."

"Take off your shirt."

Benito did not comply. It took Bobby Joe, Umberto and Felix to get his arms behind him and bind his wrists with two zip ties.

"Take his shirt off," Hans-Peter said.

Felix and Umberto tore the shirt off Benito, pulled it out from under the straps of his overalls. Bobby Joe patted Benito's pockets but not his chest. He poked Benito on the faint tattoo still visible on his rib cage. The tattoo was a bell suspended from a fishhook.

Hans-Peter nodded. "Ten Bells thief school."

"Some foolishness from my youth. You can see it has faded away."

"Felix, he belongs to Don Ernesto," Hans-Peter said. "You hired him, Felix. You and Bobby Joe can take him for a ride."

From the crab boat, Captain Marco saw Benito's shirt torn off, saw Bobby Joe's gun. He took out his cell phone.

A half mile up the street Antonio in his pool truck answered the call.

"Antonio, one of Schneider's pendejos pulled on Benito. We've got to get him out. I'm going to the dock and cover him if he jumps in the water."

"I'm going after him," Antonio said.

Antonio pushed the old truck hard. It was not far to the bus stop where weary gardeners and maids were waiting to start the slow ride home. Antonio got out. Several of the people waiting greeted him by name.

"Transporte libre!" Antonio called to them. "Estoy celebrando! Voy a transportar cada uno de ustedes a su casa! A ride directly to your house! No dinero, no transfer. Vengan conmigo! Vamos a parar en Yumbo Buffet. Podemos comer todo lo que queremos! Plus takeout! A free ride to your doorstep. All you can eat on the way! Todo libre!!"

"Antonio, no manejas borracho?"

"No, no. I have not had a drink. I invite you to smell me. Come on!"

The bus riders piled into Antonio's pool service truck. Two in the cab with him and three in back.

"First we pick up one more," Antonio said.

Cari Mora was upstairs in the house with a six-pack of toilet paper and some lightbulbs. The bedrooms were a piggish mess, towels and a copy of *Juggs Triple DDD* skin magazine on the bathroom floor. The one made-up bed had some lewd comic books and the five parts of a field-stripped AK-47 scattered on it. A lube can oozed onto the coverlet beside two loaded banana clips. She picked up the lube can with two fingers and put it on the dresser.

Her telephone buzzed. Antonio calling.

"Cari, take cover. Get ready to bail. They got a gun on Benito. I'm coming after him. Marco's coming to the dock." He was gone.

Cari looked down from the high bedroom window. She saw Bobby Joe poke Benito with the muzzle of a pistol.

Slap slap click click—Cari put the gas tube on the AK-47.

When she pushed the hammer down with her thumb and held it out of the way with the trigger, the bolt and bolt carrier slid in easily, then the wavy recoil spring and dust cover. Function check. She inserted a banana clip and jacked a round into the chamber.

Locked and loaded in forty-five seconds. She went back to the window. The front sight of the rifle covered the bump on the back of Bobby Joe's head. The front gate was swinging open.

As Antonio drove in the gate he called Captain Marco on the boat, put his phone on speaker and dropped the phone into his breast pocket.

Antonio could see Umberto putting three concrete blocks and some baling wire into the back of Felix's truck. Benito stood beside the truck with Bobby Joe and Felix. Benito's hands were behind him, probably cuffed, Antonio thought. Antonio drove close. He got out of the truck and approached the old man.

Seeing Antonio's truck crowded with people, Bobby Joe held his gun behind his hip.

"Hey, Benito! Hey, señor! I'm supposed to take you home," Antonio said. "I'm sorry I forgot."

"We're taking him home," Felix said.

All of Antonio's passengers were watching.

"No, señor," Antonio said loudly. "I promised his Lupe to get him home for supper completely sober."

A laugh from the people crowded into the truck. A few of them were puzzled, almost positive Lupe had been dead for years.

"She'll kill me if I don't show up with him." Antonio turned to his passengers. "Will or will not Lupe kill me?"

"Sí," said several in the truck. "Cierto. Definitely. Lupe will kill you, as she has killed all others who gave him the chance to drink."

Bobby Joe came up beside Antonio and muttered, "Get the fuck out of here."

"Shoot me in front of the jury, butt breath," Antonio said softly.

Hans-Peter Schneider came out on the front steps. Bobby Joe and Felix looked to him. Schneider gave them a small shake of the head. Felix sidled behind Benito and cut the handcuff strips. Hans-Peter Schneider came down the steps and gave Benito a sizable roll of bills.

"We'll need you in two weeks, comprendes? I give

you another like this. There is no reason we cannot work together."

There was much grumbling and joshing among the passengers as Benito found a seat in the back of the truck.

Antonio was talking down into his pocket on his telephone with Marco. "Where's Cari?"

"I've got her. She'll be coming out the back, I'm at the dock for her. Go!" Marco said.

Antonio backed the truck toward the gate. Hans-Peter held his hands out, palms turned back toward his men.

"Let them go," Hans-Peter said.

Cari ran down the winding stairs carrying the rifle. She encountered nobody. She took the bird out of its cage and put it on her shoulder. "You better hold on. And leave my earrings alone," she said, backing across the yard toward the dock where the crab boat waited, pressing with its bow hard enough to shake the dock.

She passed the rifle to Marco in the bow and jumped for the deck, the bird flapping. The crab boat backed away with a great thrashing, Marco with the gun covering the blank rear windows, seeing nobody.

Antonio drove away from the house, the gate swinging shut behind the loaded truck.

"Your shirt is a disgrace," the man sitting on the spare tire told Benito. "They will never allow you in Yumbo Buffet."

CHAPTER EIGHT

Captain Marco sat with Benito and Antonio under the open shed. A single high floodlight shone down on the boatyard. Five minutes of rain and they could smell the wet ground. Runoff from the roof tapped a line in the dirt.

"You think Felix is working both sides of the street?" Captain Marco said.

Benito shrugged. "Probably. He could have asked me like a man to be silent, paid me an honorable sum—but he had to show me his knife. I think his knife would fit into his asshole, but loosely, with room for his sunglasses."

"To speak further of holes, this one under the patio goes back all the way under Pablo's house?" Captain Marco said.

"I don't know, but it's deep. The sea dug where the

FBI did not. You can hear it sucking, it's open to the bay underwater at the base of the seawall."

Big moths flew around a bare bulb above the men. One lit on Antonio's head. Its feet tickled his forehead until he fanned it away.

Captain Marco poured a short round of rum and squeezed a lime into his glass.

"How long have they got the house?"

"There's a thirty-day filming permit posted on the gate," Antonio said. "It was issued to Alexander Smoot of Smoot Productions."

Benito rubbed a lime on the rim of his glass. The rum was Flor de Caña 18 and the taste of it made him close his eyes for a happy second, tasting it off Lupe's mouth from moons ago as though she were here in this moment.

When the men saw Cari Mora coming out of the boatyard office, Benito made her a drink like his own and Antonio brought another cane chair to the table. She had the bird on her shoulder. The big cockatoo climbed off onto the top of the chair. She passed it a grape from a bowl on the table.

"Touch it, Mamacita!" the bird said, a reference to an earlier venue in its checkered life.

"Shh," she said, and gave the bird another grape.

"Cari, you have to stay well clear of that place," Benito said. "Hans-Peter will sell you, do you know that? He will never believe you are not with us."

"I know."

"Does he have any idea where you stay, away from that house?"

"No, and neither does Felix."

"Do you need a place to stay?" Benito said.

"I have an extra room," Antonio said quickly.

"I'm okay. I have a place," she said.

Captain Marco tapped the building plans on the table.

"Cari, do you know what's going on here?"

"They made some holes in the walls and they're tearing up the basement looking for something," she said. "It's not hard to imagine what it is. Clearly you look for it too."

"Do you know who we are?"

"Probably. To me you are my friends Señor Benito and Antonio and Captain Marco. That's all I want to know."

"You can be in or out," Captain Marco said.

"I am out, but I want you to win," Cari said. "Maybe I can tell you what little I know and maybe you don't tell me secrets I have to keep."

"What did you see in the house?"

"Hans-Peter Schneider got in a couple of yelling matches on the phone with somebody that he called Jesús. He used a phone card to call Colombia. Mucha lucha. He kept asking, 'Where is it?' They swept with metal detectors from the attic down. Lot of rebar in the foundations, they drilled a couple of times. They had a big magnetic drill press, like eighty pounds, and two air hammers."

"What were you supposed to think with them tearing the place up?"

"Felix said don't worry, it was his responsibility as rental agent. I said write that down. He said no. The one Schneider flashed some money. To me, quite a lot of money."

"Did he pay you?"

"Oh, no. He just waved it around and gave me grocery money. I have a new text here from Felix. He says: *The boss does not want you some more, but you can come get your money. Or we will send it to your home when you give us the address, or meet you with it at my earliest convenience....* Right, I'll jump on that."

"Did anybody see you leaving the house?"

"I don't think so but I'm not sure. I think they were all in the front."

"They've missed the gun," Marco said. "Maybe they will see it again."

"I'll go now," Cari said.

Antonio got up quickly. "Wait a little while, Cari, and I'll take you to wherever you may or may not be staying for all we know."

"There's a comfortable seat out on the dock," Marco said.

Antonio carried her drink out for her and went back to the table.

"Schneider has to be careful now," Captain Marco said. "The federales see him digging in Miami Beach, they'll be on him like a man falling out of a tree."

Marco unrolled some building plans on the table and weighted them down with the bottle and a coconut.

"Pablo's lawyer filed this plan with the city to get the permit years ago when they built the patio," the captain said. "See, it's on concrete piers. That's why it didn't collapse when the sea dug it out underneath. You saw the picture Felix took?"

"Just over his shoulder," Benito said. "He was hugging it to his chicken chest. I have this one. What can you expect from a flip phone?"

"How big was the box you saw?"

The old gardener put his lumpy finger on the building plan. "The box was about here. For scale I only have the skull beside it in this dim picture. The box is bigger than a big refrigerator. Like the big ice machine at Casablanca Fish Market."

"That big a cave, the hole under the seawall may be big too," Antonio said.

"Big enough to drag out a big ice machine?" the captain said.

"Nacho Nepri could do it from his barge with

the big winch," Antonio said. "He moves pieces of riprap bigger than that with his winch and crane. If we could get him to do it."

"We need to see the hole under the seawall. How much water you got there at high tide?" the captain said.

"Along there, eight feet," Antonio said. "I can look at it underwater from the bay side."

"You want to go off the crab boat?"

"No, I can get into a place down the street where I do the pool. I'd rather slide along the seawall from there."

"Tomorrow ebb tide starts half an hour before sunset," Marco said. "The forecast is clear. Bad glare off the bay into their faces and most likely a raft of grass on the tide. Don't go in the hole, Antonio. Just slide in there under the grass and take a look. You got air?"

Antonio nodded and rose to leave.

The old gardener lifted a glass to him. "Antonio. Gracias for the ride today."

"De nada," Antonio said.

"Though I thought my bill at Yumbo Buffet was excessive for all those people in the truck," Benito said. "After stuffing their faces, they shamelessly ordered to go, with three gaseosas to wash it down. Antonio…escúchame joven: You will have to watch it now. Bobby Joe will be looking for you."

"If Bobby Joe's luck is really bad, he will find me," Antonio said.

Captain Marco went home to his spare efficiency near the boatyard.

Benito fired up his old pickup and rattled off home. They left a fire in the incinerator, the door open for the firelight.

Lupe was waiting at Benito's house, in spirit, in the small garden she had made behind Benito's house. He felt her presence warm and close to him as fireflies winked over the white blossoms, luminous under the moon. Benito poured a glass of Flor de Caña for himself and one for her. He drank both of them sitting in the garden with Lupe, and being there together was enough.

Cari and Antonio sat on an old car seat on the boatyard dock and looked up at the sky. The bass thump of some distant music came across the water.

"What do you want?" Antonio said. "What would you like to have?"

"I want to live in a place that belongs to me," Cari said, biting the lime and dropping it back in her drink. "A house where every place you put your hand down is clean. And you can walk around barefooted and the floor feels good."

"Live by yourself?"

She shrugged and nodded. "If my cousin had a good place too, and some help with her mom. I want my own house. Close the door and it's a sweet quiet. Keep it up yourself. You can hear rain on the roof and you know it's not dripping in on the foot of the bed, it's running off into the garden."

"Garden now."

"Cómo no? I'd like to have some little place to plant stuff. Go out and pick something green and cook it. Steam a snapper in a banana leaf. Play loud music in the kitchen when I want to and maybe have a drink while I'm cooking, dance around in front of the stove."

"A guy? You want a guy?"

"I want to own the front door. Then maybe I invite somebody in it."

"Say I showed up on the front steps and knocked. Like, you know, Single Antonio shows up."

"You gonna be Single Antonio, Antonio? Antonio Soltero Antonio?" The rum felt pretty good.

"No, I'm not going to be Antonio Soltero. Not now. If I do that, somebody's got to leave the country. I'm not doing that. I got my citizenship serving in the Marines. She can't get hers that way anymore. She's got to wait. She's my friend so I wait with her. Her brother was with me in the service. We lost him." Antonio tapped the globe and anchor tattoo on his arm. "Semper Fi."

"Semper Fi is a good one. But that's just one of your tattoos."

"The Ten Bells? I was a kid. It was a different kind of school. Different set of skills. I don't have to justify to you."

"True that."

"I'll just say, when I get my business straight, like, to suit you? You will have to burn the front steps out from under me."

Music from the dark ships up and down the river where televisions glowed. Now Rodrigo Amarante's strange and beautiful theme from *Narcos*. More conga than tune reached them across the water.

Antonio had a voice he thought was pretty good. He looked directly at her and sang along.

I am the fire that burns your skin,
I am the water that kills your thirst…
I am the castle tower,
The sword that guards the flowing spring.

For a moment a ship's horn drowned him out.

You are the air I breathe
And the light of the moon on the sea.

Clouds passed under the moon, painting the moving river in patches of soot and silver. For a moment the river looked easy to wade in.

Sparks flew upward from the fire.

Cari rose and kissed Antonio on the top of his head. He turned his face up to her just too late.

"I need to go home, Antonio Soltero," she said.

CHAPTER NINE

Cari's only family in Miami were her elderly aunt Jasmín, her cousin Julieta, and Julieta's baby.

When Cari did not have a live-in job, she stayed with them in a housing project near Claude Pepper Way in Miami. Julieta's husband had been seized by Immigration and Customs Enforcement when he went in voluntarily to register as instructed. He was in Krome Detention Center awaiting deportation for bouncing a check.

Like many Miamians who arrived in the U.S. on foot, Cari kept her business to herself. Only Marco and Antonio knew about her cousin, or where Julieta lived.

Late in the evening she let herself in the back door of the building with her key. Cari's aunt and her cousin and the baby were asleep. She checked on Aunt Jasmín, bedridden, tiny and brown against the sheets. She looked at her aunt's sleeping face. Jasmín's eyes opened, pupils big and fathomless looking at Cari. Cari felt engulfed in her gaze. She could see in her aunt's features vague resemblances to her mother's face, as she sometimes saw familiar shapes in clouds. She felt that Jasmín was trying to tell her a secret, trying to recall something important to tell her, something only old people understood, though Cari knew very well there was nobody home in there.

Cari had the smell of the gun on her hands. She scrubbed them with lime juice and soap before she sat beside the sleeping baby, listening to her breathe. Cari had not smelled gun oil for a long time or tasted the copper taste of war, like a penny under her tongue...

At the age of eleven Cari had been taken from her village at gunpoint and conscripted into FARC, the Fuerzas Armadas Revolucionarias de Colombia.

FARC trained her as a soldier, and took her picture as a child soldier of the New Colombia. They jammed the regulation subdural contraceptive into her upper arm and used her in the ways that she was useful—she was quick and dexterous and strong. Cari was a child among children in the guerrilla base deep in the Caquetá forest.

They made it like a camp at first, for the little ones. The officers told the children they could go home in two weeks if they did not like the army. But truly they could never go home.

The children played together when they were not training. Many came from broken homes and were grateful for any attention. When the air raids stopped there was dancing in the camp at night. Sex among the teens was not frowned on, but marriage and pregnancy were forbidden. Abortion was mandatory. The officers told them they were married to the revolution.

Music and colored lights seemed magical to many of the little ones, coming as they did from remote villages.

And then, a month in, during a party in the trees at night, a couple tried to run away. They were thirteen years old and this was the second offense. The pickets caught them wading away in the shallows of the Caquetá River. The lookouts held them there in the flashlights and sent word to the camp. Everyone was assembled on the riverbank.

The comandante made a speech, lights flashing on his little round glasses. There had been a number of desertions recently and it had to stop. The two young people shivered in the beams of the flashlights, their legs trembling, their clothing wet, their hands tied behind them with white zip-tie strips.

The girl's clothing, wet and clinging, revealed a small baby bump. A bundle of food they had taken was on the ground beside them. Their hands bound, the boy and girl could not hold each other. They stood close and pressed the sides of their heads together.

The comandante said how wrong it was to desert. Should they be punished? "Judge them," he said. "Should they be punished? They deserted you and they took your food. Hold up your hand if you think they should be punished."

All the adults and most of the child soldiers thought yes, they should be punished. Cari held up her small hand with the others. Yes, they should be punished. Spanked perhaps? No breakfast even? Kitchen Patrol with Cari? The comandante signaled with his hand. The guards pushed the boy and girl into the shallows and shot them. The guards seemed hesitant to shoot at first. No one wanted to shoot first. The comandante barked. A shot, two, and then a lot of shots. The children went facedown, and rolled face up, and facedown again, blood in the water around them, and floated slowly away. One of the guards pushed the dead girl with his foot when her body stopped against a root. The ends of the white tie strips stuck out far from their small wrists. They floated away facedown, side by side, blood on the water like a scarf around them. Cari cried. Most of the children screamed and cried.

They could hear the radio back at the camp still playing dance music.

How small the dead children's wrists were. How far the ends of the tie strips stuck out from their small wrists. When Cari heard the word "horrible," that is where her mind went.

Zip ties were everywhere, for a while they were the fashion for both the guerrillas and their enemies, the paramilitaries: a row of zip ties on a web belt ready to bind a prisoner. Zip ties do not rot and they shine whiter than the bones of skeletons on the jungle floor. Coming upon a corpse in the bush, it was not the rotting face that turned Cari's stomach, or the buzzards flapping away, heavy from their meal. It was the bright zip tie that bound the wrists. The guerrillas trained with them—how to bind a prisoner using one hand to fasten the zip ties, how to shim a zip tie to escape, how to cut them with shoelaces. Bound wrists appeared a lot in Cari's dreams.

Not tonight, not this night in Miami, in a chair beside the baby in her cousin's home. She had seen from the window the zip tie cut from Benito's wrists and seen the old man leave alive.

She did not think of other things. She listened to the baby breathing and drifted off to sleep.

Chapter Ten

Barranquilla, Colombia

Clínica Ángeles de la Misericordia, where Jesús Villarreal lay, is a hospital for the poor on a crowded market street. At midday a black Range Rover came to a stop in front of the hospital. The street crowd and vendors' carts streamed around the car, vendors arguing and jostling for space.

Isidro Gomez, large and florid, got out of the front passenger seat. With nothing but the lift of his chin, he cleared space at the curb for the car. Gomez opened the rear door. His boss got out.

Don Ernesto Ibarra, forty-four, known to the tabloids as "Don Teflon," is a man of medium height wearing a pressed linen bush jacket.

A number of patients in the hospital recognized Don Ernesto at once and called out his name as he and Gomez passed among them, through the stark ground-floor ward with its worn linoleum floor and the beds divided by screens.

Jesús Villarreal's room was one of two private rooms at the end of the ward. Gomez went in without knocking. In a minute he came back out, rubbing his hands with an antiseptic wipe. He nodded to Don Ernesto, who went inside.

Jesús Villarreal lay in the bed, a withered old man, caught alive in the trap of rails and tubes around him. He tugged the oxygen mask away from his face.

"You were always careful, Don Ernesto," Jesús Villarreal said. "You search the dying now? You send this enormous man to grope people in their beds?"

The Don smiled at him. "You shot at me in Cali."

"It was just business, and you were shooting back," Jesús said.

"I still regard you as a dangerous man, Jesús. Take it as a compliment. We can go forward in friendship."

"You are an educator, Don Ernesto, an academic. You teach better ways to steal. But they don't teach friendship at the school of Ten Bells."

Don Ernesto considered Jesús, shrunken in the hospital bed. Looking at the old man, Don Ernesto tilted and turned his head as a crow might do examining a berry on the ground.

"Your future is short, Jesús. You called me, and I came because I respect you. You were Pablo's captain, you never sold him out, yet he left you nothing. Let us use the time you have and talk like men."

The old man took a few breaths of oxygen from the mask to supplement the tube in his nose. He spoke in bursts.

"In 1989 I took gold to Miami for Pablo under ice in my trawler. A half ton of gold with fish on top—some groupers and a lot of sheepsheads. Thirty gold bars of the kind they call Good Delivery, four hundred troy ounces each, cast with numbers. Twenty-five kilo bars as well, the flat shape, but of doré gold from the mines at Inirida. And a big bag of tola bars of one hundred seventeen grams, I don't know how many." Jesús rested a minute, sucking air. "A thousand pounds of gold. I can tell you where it is. Do you know how much is worth a thousand pounds of gold?"

"About twenty-five million dollars U.S."

"What will you give me?"

"What do you want?"

"Money and safety for Adriana and the boy."

Don Ernesto nodded. "Claro. You know that my word is good."

"Without offense, Don Ernesto, my policy is cash and carry."

"With equal courtesy I ask you who else you have sold this information to other than Hans-Peter Schneider."

"It is too late for us to play catch-me, fuck-me," Jesús said. "He has found the vault that holds the gold. He cannot open it and stay alive unless I tell him how. Maybe Hans-Peter Schneider will try to move the whole thing to a remote place."

"Can he move it and live?"

"Perhaps not."

"Does it have a mercury switch? Will it blow up if it's moved?"

Jesús Villarreal only pursed his lips. His lips were cracked and painful to purse.

"You can tell me how to open it," Don Ernesto said.

"Yes. I will tell you now about some difficulties, and when you come with *dinero efectivo* in hand we will discuss how to solve them."

CHAPTER ELEVEN

Dust from Africa carried on the wind colored the Miami dawn pink. On the far shore of Biscayne Bay, windows flared orange as the sun heaved out of the sea.

Hans-Peter Schneider and Felix stood on the patio of the Escobar house beside the hole in the lawn.

Umberto had made the hole bigger with a pick and a spade. From the dark below them came sucking noises. As the sea pulsed through the opening under the seawall and into the cave beneath them, the hole breathed out foul air. They turned their faces away from the stench.

Bobby Joe and Mateo brought some equipment out of the pool house.

A stacked echelon of pelicans passed over, heading for a fish drive.

"The fuck can I know what Jesús told Don Ernesto?" Schneider said. "We take it out the front, out the back, I could care less. What about the guy in Lauderdale?"

"Clyde Hopper, the engineer," Felix said. "He's got the equipment. He'll meet us and work it out. He wants a meet at the boat."

"Is his number on this telephone?" Hans-Peter said. He tapped his palm with the blue burner phone from the trunk of Felix's car.

"What is that? I don't know," Felix said. He licked his lips.

"It's the phone from the trunk of your car. Tell me the code to open the phone or Bobby Joe will blow your brains out."

"Star six nine six nine. It's just to talk to my girl-friend without the wife—you know."

Hans-Peter pursed his lips as he poked the tele-phone and confirmed the code. He could explore the phone later.

"Okey-dokey," Hans-Peter said. "Okey-dokey. Maybe we won't need to pull it out, this fucking thing. Maybe we can crack it from the back. We're going into the hole to look."

"Who's going into the hole?" Felix said.

Standing behind Felix were Bobby Joe and Mateo. Umberto was with them and he was holding a har-ness.

The line from the harness ran through a pulley on a big limb of the sea grape tree above the hole and on to a winch, a hand-cranked coffin hoist.

Bobby Joe held up the harness.

"Put it on," Schneider told Felix.

"I didn't sign up for this," Felix said. "Anything happens to me you got trouble with my office."

"You signed up for any fucking thing I tell you to do," Schneider said. "You think you're the only one in your office with their hand stuck out?"

Bobby Joe strapped Felix into the harness and hooked it to the line. Felix kissed a medal he wore around his neck.

Hans-Peter stood in front of Felix to have a pleasant little sip of Felix's fear before the mask covered the man's face.

It was a hazmat mask with two big charcoal filters on the cheeks, and headgear with a video camera and a miner's light. Attached to his harness were a big flashlight and a large holster. Felix was wired for sound.

It was hard for him to suck enough air through the filters of the mask.

Birds passed across the sky, crows mobbing a hawk. Felix looked up and thought *I love the sky*. He had never thought about it before. His legs felt weak. "Give me a gun," he said.

Bobby Joe put a big revolver in the holster and

snapped the flap over it. "Don't put your hand on the gun until you are under the ground," he said.

They lowered Felix into the hole. The air below-ground felt warm on his legs. He spun a little, hanging on the cable.

Once his head was below the grass it was hard to see. Daylight coming down through the hole reflected very little off the rough concrete of the seawall. Gloom became black darkness as the cave stretched away. The distance from the surface of the water to the ceiling varied from six feet to four feet as the water surged in the cave. When Felix was submerged to his waist, his feet found the bottom. The water swelled and fell from his hips to his chest and back again. The snaky roots of the sea grape came down through the ceiling. The roots were too stiff to push aside. Felix's light bounced off the water and threw big shadows of the roots. He could see in patches the underside of the concrete patio and hanging dirt above him.

Hans-Peter Schneider watched on a laptop, Felix's voice tinny on the speakers.

"The bottom's pretty flat, I can walk. Water's up to my chest. Shit—that's half a dog!"

"You are doing just fine, Felix. Go look at the fucking cube," Schneider said. "Do it now."

Felix moved slowly toward the back of the cave.

The pilings supporting the patio were around him like the pillars of a flooded temple. He was sweating. The light on his head reached the shelving beach and reflected off metal. His big flashlight revealed the beach was littered with bones, and a single human skull. The cube was big all right.

"It's a box, taller than it is wide. Steel diamond plate, like a nonslip floor. Edges are welded."

"How big?" Schneider said.

"Size of a refrigerator, bigger, like a deli refrigerator."

"Any lifting rings? Handles?"

"I can't see."

"Well go up close and look at it."

A fizzing sound behind Felix. He turned toward the sound. He saw concentric rows of small bubbles rising in a coffin shape.

Felix scrambled onto the beach.

"No handles, no lift rings, no door, no lid. I can't see all of it, there's dirt around some of it."

A fizzing noise and Felix swung his light around. A pair of eyes reflected red in the dark water. He fired the pistol toward the eyes and they disappeared.

"I'm coming out, I'm coming out." He waded fast to get back under the hole in the ceiling of the cave. "Pull me up! Pull me up."

The winch was turning, the line was moving in

front of him, the line was out of the water, dripping. The winch took up the slack and Felix was beginning to rise when a tremendous jerk moved him sideways and he went down in the water, the flashlight flying from his hand, the pistol fired into the ceiling.

Up in the garden the winch spun backward, the handle whacking Bobby Joe on the hands and arms, whirring as the line paid out, the line slithering fast down the hole.

Down in the cave the line slithered out the hole under the seawall, came taut and sang, throwing drops of water. Then it fell limp to the floor of the cave.

"Crank him up!" Schneider yelled.

Watching the laptop, Schneider could see through Felix's head camera the sea floor passing underneath him, the miner's light beam bouncing along the bottom. Mateo and Umberto worked the winch, raising the harness.

It came out of the hole containing the lower half of Felix, his lower torso and legs draped with loops of pink and gray intestine.

In the distance, out on the bay, Felix's hand broke the surface, cutting the water in something like a wave, until it was pulled down out of sight.

The men were quiet for a minute.

"That was my fucking pistol," Bobby Joe said.

Umberto tried on Felix's hat and his shades. "What about the house?" Umberto said.

Hans-Peter took the shades back from Umberto.

"A person in Felix's office admires the glasses," he said. "You can keep the hat."

CHAPTER TWELVE

Early in the morning Cari was grating carrots for the salsa picante Julieta sold at the farmers' market.

The big white cockatoo muttered on its perch, annoyed by the crowing of roosters in the neighborhood.

"Chupa huevos," the bird said.

Like Cari, Julieta was licensed as a home health aide—a handy skill now that her mother was housebound with no medical benefits.

They had furnished Julieta's small apartment with oversize northern furniture given to them by families of elderly patients they had nursed to the end. Families of the sick liked the two young women very much; they were cheerful, strong enough to lift the patient, and they could look at anything without it showing on their faces. The furniture was comfortable but they had to climb around it in the small apartment.

On the living room wall was an attractive poster for a concert in Tel Aviv in 1958, in the hall a photograph of Julieta in a bikini, being crowned Miss Hawaiian Tropic.

From the back bedroom Julieta called to Cari over the crying of the infant. "Cari, would you warm a bottle?"

Cari's cell phone rang. She had to dry her hands on her apron to fish it out of her purse. Antonio was calling.

He was in his truck. "Cari, listen to me. How would you like to make four hundred bucks today?" He held the phone away from his ear for a second. "Excuse me? I beg your pardon, señorita, this is not monkey business. Negocio legítimo, totalmente. Tu sabes que soy un hombre de mi palabra. I need you to help me, Cari. Late this afternoon I'm going to look under—you know, I'm just going to take a look. Come help me."

CHAPTER THIRTEEN

With the prospect of gainful employment in the afternoon, Cari splurged; instead of riding the bus she took an UberX to North Miami Beach, paying $9.21.

The house was near the Snake Creek Canal in a neighborhood of small neat homes hard-won by their owners. Most families managed to have in their gardens a mango tree and a papaya, a Meyer lemon maybe.

This was the only house in disrepair, a repo entangled with the bank, its owner dragged out by ICE and deported in the middle of the night. It had been vacant for five years. Each side in the estate dispute enjoined the other from fixing it up. It had its own mango tree in the backyard, but the tree was struggling and badly in need of pruning and feed.

Cari had spotted the house months before and copied the information off the sign in the front yard. Her first visit had been conducted by a disinterested bank underling. The man let her into the house and waited in the car, drinking a TruMoo and drumming his pale soft fingers on the wheel. He had already told his supervisor that Cari "didn't have a Chinaman's chance of getting a mortgage." He honked to hurry her along.

This time Cari came to the house alone.

She brought some Vigoro fruit tree fertilizer from Home Depot. The gate to the side yard had sagged on its hinges and was not locked. She pushed it open.

Cari sat on a plastic milk crate in the overgrown back garden of the vacant house and looked at the mango tree. She put her hand on the tree. The breeze touched Cari's hair and whispered in the mango. She applied the fertilizer, careful not to get any on the trunk. Mangoes do not like fertilizer on their trunks.

The woman who lived next door, hearing the creaking gate, watched Cari through a low hole in the fence. When she saw Cari feed the mango tree her face relaxed. The woman came over and offered Cari her ladder if she wanted to look into the attic. Cari went inside the house.

The sun shone through a hole in the roof into the bedroom. The second bedroom was half painted, the paint complete on one wall and petering out on a second wall, winding down to a stiff paintbrush left on the floor, where the painter had finished drinking his bottle of weak-knee. The empty bottle lay beside the paintbrush on the matted and curling carpet. The house had good tile floors.

There was a little vandalism—OGALVY CAN KISS MY BUT was written on an inner wall at a child's eye level along with a rude drawing, presumably Ogalvy with jackass ears, but there were no crack vials on the floor or food wrappers. The smell of mold came from behind the rain-streaked wallboard. The commode rocked on its base.

Cari thought the house was wonderful.

Bad news in the attic. Some trusses rotting. A nest woven from grass and insulation was in the corner of the attic over the kitchen. Cari knelt on the beams and looked at the abandoned nest. Rat? Nope, a possum—no doubt about it. The nest bag had the hallmark emergency exit on the side in addition to the formal entrance. Cari had in her time made possum soup when the grub ran out. She had been taught in the jungle to make field rat soup as a specific against whooping cough, but found the recipe tasted about the same using possums, and was equally ineffective as medicine. Cari knew how to do many things. She had no experience at replacing roofing trusses and setting roofing tiles. She knew she could learn.

A sun shower came, pelting hard on the house, drumming and crackling on the roof close over her head as she knelt on the beams. The rain came in the hole in the roof and was a glittering column down through the house in the bright sunshine. She put her hand in the rain as though she could keep it out of the house. The shower was over in minutes. Cari came outside onto the steaming ground, hoping for a rainbow. There was one.

The neighbor was tiny and very wrinkled. Her name was Teresa and she was old when she came to America from La Gomera in the Spanish Canaries. She saved cell phone minutes by communicating with her sister two blocks away with Silbo Gomero whistle talk. Teresa offered Cari two mangoes off her own tree. She put them in a bright orange bag from Sabor Tropical.

Among the neighbors, Teresa explained without prompting, the Prieto mango was most popular with households of Cuban origin, such as the Vargases, whose son was in dental school. The Madame Francis mango was favored among those from Haiti, like the Toussaints on the corner, whose daughter was starting law school. The Neelam mango was preferred by the Vidyapatis, a Hindu family of pari-mutuel clerks from India at the end of the street, whose son was a medical student at U of M, she went on. The Jamaicans were extremely opinionated and scoffed at all this in favor of the Julie mango. They were the Higginses, whose daughter was a pharmacist now. The Chinese were divided in their opinions and used all types of mango mixed with lychee in their Café Canton on 163rd Street. *Their* son Weldon Wing had been regarded by the elders as a nincompoop because he went around singing all the time and performed at open-mic nights as the rapper "Love-Jones." But Weldon, or Love-Jones, rose swiftly in his family's regard when he got his own fried-chicken franchise from Popeyes, which the neighbor gave the Miami pronunciation of "Popayez."

They heard a whistle, thin and clear, from far away. It went on for several seconds, up and down.

"Excuse me," the neighbor said. "Do I have any vacuum cleaner bags indeed!"

She stuck two fingers in her mouth and whistled a phrase so loudly Cari had to step back.

"I guess I told her," the tiny woman said. "She is forever borrowing my vacuum cleaner bags. I suggested she go to Walmart, where they have them for sale. You want this house? I will pray for you. I can squirt water on the mango through the peephole in the fence."

Chapter Fourteen

A half hour before sunset Antonio's pool service truck pulled into a driveway a block and a half from the Escobar mansion. Cari Mora was driving.

"I do the pool for these people every week," Antonio said. "They won't be back in Miami Beach until the end of September."

He got out and punched in the gate code.

The gate swung very slowly, Cari thought. She wanted to ask Antonio the code in case she had to open it without him. She didn't want to ask.

He saw it in her face. "From the inside it opens when you drive close to it." He waved her in. She turned the truck around in the courtyard until it faced the gate.

"Wait here until you see me, or I call you."

She got out of the truck and stood with him.

"What if you get a problem? I can help you," she said. "I can swim with you. We can put the pistol in the ziplock bag and I can cover you from under the dock next door. I could keep them off the seawall if they see you."

"Nope," Antonio said. "Thank you, Cari, I invited you to help me—we do this my way, okay?"

"Antonio, it's better if I cover you."

"You want to do this my way, Cari, or do you want to go home? Just think about your business, I'll think about my business. Stay with the truck. Listen to me—if I have to come out of the water down the street, I'll call you." He held up a cell phone in a ziplock bag. "If there are guys in the street with me, come fast. Stop with the bed of the truck beside me. I'll jump in the back. You haul ass and get us out of there. Don't worry. I'll be right back here in thirty minutes at the most."

He took his scuba gear out of the back of the truck.

Antonio looked at Cari and saw some color in her cheeks. He reached in the glove box and got out an envelope.

"These are the tickets to see Juanes at the Hard Rock. If you won't go with Wicked Old Antonio, take your cousin." He winked at her and walked around the house and out of sight without looking back.

Antonio put on his tank and mask under cover

of a hedge. In the distance he could see the honeymoon ships making smoke in Government Cut. Being with Cari had Antonio a little steamed up and he thought probably the honeymoon ships' engines weren't even running and the smoke came off the bedrooms.

The sky was bright orange in the west, the light off the water swarming on the underside of the sea grape trees in patches the size of his hand.

Antonio went down the ladder from the dock of the vacant house and slid into the water. He spit in his mask and rubbed it around. His camera was strapped to his wrist.

He swam 150 yards along the seawall, going under the docks, staying about six feet under the surface. He came up under the dock next door to the Escobar house. Reflections from the lowering sun shivered light under the dock. He had to be careful of nails sticking down through the boards. A spiderweb caught in his hair. He submerged for a moment in case the spider was on his head. Rafts of grass littered with foam cups and plastic water bottles slid by on the tide with a bobbing palm frond as long as an alligator. The lid of a cooler floated past him, shielding several small fish from the sky.

They were grinding in the basement of the Escobar house. Mateo and the crew were peeling plaster and cement off the basement wall. It was hard going. They had an air hammer, chisels, pry bars and a Sawzall. Dust was thick in the air.

Hans-Peter Schneider watched from the stairs, wiping his pale skull with an embroidered handkerchief.

They had started at the top and in half a day they had peeled down far enough to reveal first a halo, then the countenance of a holy figure, a woman painted on the landward face of the cube. The figure looked at them over the cracked plaster and cement. Mateo recognized her. He crossed himself. "Nuestra Señora de Caridad del Cobre," he said.

In the waterside garden of the Escobar house Bobby Joe could not look westward over the water without shielding his eyes from the setting sun. Flocks of ibises passed over, heading home to the rookery on Bird Key. Bobby Joe shot at the flocks a few times with an air rifle, hoping to break a wing and have a bird to play with, but did not hit anything. Up on the second-floor terrace Umberto sat in a chair with his forearms on the railing, his AR-15 beside him.

The setting sun made the house glow orange, and the clouds were beginning to light up.

Bobby Joe tried to shoot a fish with his crossbow, but it ducked under the raft of grass. Bobby Joe cursed the blinding sun.

*   *   *

Under the raft of floating grass Antonio approached the Escobar seawall, staying in the patch of gloom that moved over the rough bottom of riprap and silt. He was about six feet down. A school of mullet passed him, dark silver under the shadows and bright silver again as they went out into the sun. Two cormorants passed over him, swimming hard after the fish.

A big cruiser came down the bay about fifty yards out, moving too fast through the manatee zone, throwing a big wake. There were girls on the foredeck and one on the fantail. The girls on the foredeck were bare-breasted and wore only bikini bottoms.

Umberto watched from the upstairs terrace. He focused his binoculars on the girls with one hand and with the other rubbed his private parts.

He whistled to Bobby Joe on the ground.

Underwater, Antonio heard the thrumming of the boat. He hugged the shelving bottom. The wake came over and he was tumbled. The raft of grass rose and fell like a beaten carpet and one of Antonio's fins broke the surface, sticking up through the grass.

Umberto saw the fin and whistled again through two fingers to Bobby Joe and pointed. Umberto spoke into a walkie-talkie. He grabbed his assault rifle and ran for the stairs.

Bobby Joe was peeing off the seawall, hoping the girls would see him. He jumped to the ground fumbling with his fly.

Underwater, Antonio approached the hole beneath the seawall. He could see the hole. Silt and sand were lifted by the current as water pulsed back and forth through the hole and the seagrass near it waved. The hole was big all right, wider than it was high, black inside. An orange sponge grew in front of it. Antonio took a couple of pictures.

Then he saw bullet tracks down through the water, whizzing by close.

Umberto and Bobby Joe were standing on the seawall. They fired several bursts into the raft of grass, fans of bullet tracks hissing through the water, the actions of the guns clacking louder than the muffled shots. Bobby Joe ran for his crossbow.

Antonio was bleeding from his leg, the cloud of blood red and then gray in the water. The hole loomed before him. Bullet tracks in the water. He turned sideways to the seawall, trying to stay deep.

Bobby Joe on the seawall saw bubbles rising through the raft of grass. Gleeful, he pointed his crossbow and fired. The line attached to the crossbow bolt tightened and water flew off it.

Antonio's fins stopped moving. Above him the raft of grass heaved on the swells, heaved like Antonio's chest.

Cari, waiting in the truck a block and a half away, had her eyes fixed on her watch.

When forty minutes had passed, she called Antonio's cell phone. Antonio did not answer. She called again.

Inside the Escobar pool house a cell phone in a bloody plastic bag lay on a table beside a sticky Sawzall. The phone buzzed and moved sideways in the bag.

Bobby Joe's bloody hand picked up the phone. He fished it out of the bag with two fingers and raised it to talk.

"Hello," Bobby Joe said.

"Antonio? Hello?" Cari said.

"Hidee-doo. Antonio has stepped away from his desk right now," Bobby Joe said. "He's giving us some head. You want to leave a message?"

Bobby Joe hung up, laughing. The men around him laughed too. Bobby Joe wiped the blood off his hands with a pool service T-shirt.

A brief sun shower came over, with big drops spattering on Antonio's truck, rattling on the roof. The rainbow that followed faded at once.

In the truck, Cari.

Her watch, ticking. Its second hand just jerking along without real ticking. The ticking was in her head. The little truck had crank windows; she cranked them down. The cool wet breeze blew through.

She felt her eyes sting, but she did not cry. Orange jasmine grew on the wall of the compound where she waited for Antonio, and she could smell the jasmine, strong after the rain.

It got away from her then and she saw her fiancé dead in the road with his groomsmen, all in the car and the car was burning, set on fire by the gunmen. Neighbors came to the church where she waited with jasmine in her hands. They came to tell her and she ran to them, ran to her fiancé. The red-haired boy was behind the wheel wearing a white lace guayabera and dead in the road. The windows of the car were starred with bullet holes and she knocked a hole in the jagged glass with a stone from the road and tried to pull him out. She reached through the broken window and tried to pull him out and held him. Brave people in the crowd tried to pull her away and she held on to him, they pulled and the glass cut furrows in her arms, and then the gas tank went off and lifted her off the ground. The blood dried brown on her wedding dress.

In her fanny pack Cari had brought a couple of meat-and-cheese baleadas in case she and Antonio got hungry. She looked at the baleadas. They were still warm and their steam had frosted the inside of their ziplock bag. She dumped them out of the pack onto the floor of the truck. She reached under the seat and got the Sig Sauer .40 and put it in the fanny pack. Cari got out of the truck. She breathed deep a couple of times as if she took strength from the jasmine. She felt light-headed.

Cari walked the block and a half to the front gate of the Escobar house. She took a bundle of flyers and junk mail from the mailbox. She would say she had come to pick up her check.

She punched in the code at the pedestrian gate. There was some space between the high hedge and the wall between the properties. Electrical conduit ran along the stone wall with breaker boxes for the yard lights and irrigation. She could walk between the hedge and the wall.

Crab-spider webs spangled with rain took light from the red sky and glowed over Cari as she passed beneath, staying close to the wall.

In the driveway Mateo was folding flat the third seat of Hans-Peter's Escalade and lining the cargo area with big plastic bags. He did not see her.

Cari stayed behind the hedge until she reached the waterside garden at the back of the house.

The threshold of the lighted pool house was smeared with drag blood. Cari left her cover and crossed the open garden. She pushed open the door to the pool house. She saw legs, she saw fins. A body lay on a banquet table in the pool house. The fins were toward her. She had seen Antonio's legs many times as he worked on the swimming pool and she had thought about them too. These were Antonio's legs. That was Antonio's torso. His head was missing.

She looked on the floor for his head, but there was nothing but a pool of blood, dark and thickening at the edges.

Her face was numb, her hands were not. She put her hand on Antonio's back. It was not cold yet.

Bobby Joe came into the pool house.

He was carrying a roll of plastic sheeting, some twine, and some hedge loppers to cut off Antonio's fingers. He had to untangle his load from the screen door and he did not see Cari for a second.

Bobby Joe was bloody down his front. When he saw Cari he dropped the plastic and grinned at her. His yellow eyes were full of her, held her entire. If he could keep her from screaming he could fuck her a couple of times before the others found out and Hans-Peter would insist on killing her. Yes, there was time to stun her for a quickie or so while she was good and warm and the rest of them could spit on their dicks and fuck her dead if they wanted to.

He got the good freezing sensation all over, raised the loppers and took the first long step and she shot him twice in the chest. Bobby Joe looked surprised until she shot him in the face.

His legs were still moving when she stepped over him. She heard shouts from the house as she stuffed the gun in the fanny pack and made a clean dive off the seawall, the grass and foam heaving like a lathered hide below her in her flight, the pouch banging against her as she hit the water, grass sticking in her hair as she plunged.

She saw movement through the green flotsam and swam hard, not coming up until she was under the dock next door, two hard breaths and under again. She saw movement long and dark through the murky water, below her and to the left. She swam as hard as she could, but the bag held her back. She was coming up for air and drew half a breath when she felt her ankle seized. She was pulled down under the water, grass in her face and hair, and she turned, wiping her face with her arm. Her other ankle was seized and she was pulled down.

She had to breathe and she fought her way up. Pulled down again. She cleared her eyes of grass; her chest was beginning to heave, she would suck in water soon. A patch of light between rafts of grass, and she could see it was Umberto in scuba gear, wide mask, bubbles coming up. He was going to drown her. Keep away from her and drown her, pulling her under by her ankles each time she tried to breathe. She got her hand inside the bag. He grabbed her ankles and she jackknifed, using his grip on her legs, and he was slow turning in his tanks.

She pressed the bag hard against him and shot

him twice through the bag, the gases blowing up inside him like a bang-stick round. She pushed against him with her feet to rise. With fire in her chest she broke the surface, sucking in spray and air, coughing and gasping. She held to a dock ladder, scraping her hands on the barnacles, and she gasped and gasped.

It was another hundred yards to the place where the truck was parked.

She sat in the truck, trembling, her hand clutching the cloth of the passenger seat. It felt under her hand like a lace guayabera, where blood dries brown.

She gasped the air thick with jasmine. She did not cry.

CHAPTER FIFTEEN

Cari Mora had two meat-and-cheese baleadas in a plastic bag, a small bottle of water, and Antonio's Sig Sauer P229 with seven rounds left in it plus a full extra clip. She had one hundred ten dollars in her wallet and the tools she used to touch up her nails on the bus. She had her short parasol, enhanced around the shaft with three lead washers off chlorine tanks. Antonio had attached the heavy washers to her parasol because she had to wait at bus stops a lot at night.

In a strip-mall parking lot Cari wiped down the inside of the truck. She could see herself in the mirrors as she wiped them. She could read nothing in her own face. She put on Antonio's hoodie in case there were security cameras. The hoodie smelled like Antonio—Mountain Air antiperspirant and a touch of chlorine. There were some rubbers in the pocket of the hoodie. She took the religious medal hanging from the mirror and dropped it in the pocket with the condoms. She left the truck and caught a bus.

A genip tree grew near the stop where she had to change buses. Clearly the owner of the fruit tree did not know what it was or recognize the food on the ground, a common circumstance in Miami. Genips lay in the grass behind the bus stop and on the sidewalk. She could see mangoes too, rotting, wasted on the ground, but they were behind a fence, too far to reach. Cari gathered two handfuls of the little genips and put them in her purse. She peeled one to suck the pulpy flesh off the seed. It had the familiar sweet-tart taste and the texture of a lychee.

Once her own cell phone rang. Antonio's telephone calling. She had seen him with his head cut off and still she had a strong urge to answer. The phone vibrated in her pocket. His phone was alive. It was not slack and still like the muscles in his back when she put her hand on him in the pool house.

She made sure her location services were off. She ate six more genips to keep her strength up. On the long bus ride to her cousin's apartment she had time to think.

If the police did not come to the Escobar house, Hans-Peter Schneider would know she could not call the police. He would think she was part of the

Ten Bells crew. Cari believed that Schneider would not bother to hunt her down until he had completed his business. Then, in his own good time, he would kill her or sell her to a place of no return.

Late in the evening she let herself in the back door of the apartment building near Claude Pepper Way. Cari's aunt and her cousin Julieta and the baby were asleep.

She rubbed her hands with the juice of a lime and scrubbed them. She sat in the room with the baby, listening to her breathe. Cari picked her up and held her when she fretted in the night. Her weary cousin Julieta heard the baby and woke.

"I got it, stay there," Cari said.

She warmed a bottle for the baby.

When the baby was wet, Cari cleaned her and powdered her and rocked her until she went back to sleep.

Late in the night she gave her own breast to her cousin's baby when she was fretful. Even with no milk the baby rubbed her head against Cari and quieted down. Cari had never done that before. It dulled her flashes of Bobby Joe's expression when she shot him in his face. Bobby Joe facedown with the back of his head blown out and the strap sticking out from the back of his cap and his legs still moving.

Rocking the infant, she looked at the stain on the ceiling shaped like Colombia. The poet was wrong, she thought. No, a baby is not just "another little house for death." No es solamente otra casita para la muerte.

She closed her eyes. She should have insisted on going in the water with Antonio. She wished she had fucked his brains out when she wanted to. She wished she had pushed through that machista nonsense and told him she was going in the water with him. Instead she let him go into a tactical situation she understood better than he did. He was a damn Marine. He knew better.

Child soldier Cari, age twelve, got demerits for inattention at indoctrination classes—the classes made no more sense to her than Sunday school—but she caught on fast to tactics. FARC found her useful.

She thought the wounded were important and she was quick to learn emergency medicine. Her hand on a soldier's face calmed the soldier while she tightened a tourniquet with the other hand.

She was good at the maintenance of weapons and equipment. Her main job, often a punishment for attitude, was cooking outdoors—twenty-gallon pots of the stew estofado de carne when they had the meat, cooking over an open fire at a place of scraped earth and camouflaged tin sheds where an Irishman was teaching them how to make mortars out of Kosan Gas cylinders, how to put a trip wire on a grenade, how to deal with a dud round in a mortar.

Kidnapping and extortion supported the guerrillas. One of Cari's duties was taking care of an older professor FARC had kidnapped. He was a naturalist and a teacher and a sometime politician, a man in delicate health from a rich family in Bogotá. She took care of him for three years. The FARC keepers were reasonably good to the old man while they received payments from his family. They gave him books looted from the mansions of the oppressor, and Cari read to him when his eyes were tired, his glasses folded in his shirt pocket. The books they would let him have were nonpolitical, his captors thought. They were poetry and horticulture and nature. A FARC officer made the professor explain Darwin to the littlest trainees as an affirmation of communism.

The FARC camp was a curious combination of old and new. Following orders, Cari made field rat soup to combat whooping cough, and at the same time the commander had a laptop computer.

One of Cari's duties was to recharge the computer's batteries, lugging the heavy battery unit or pulling it in a child's wagon to the nearest source of electricity. If the source was close and secure enough, the officers allowed the old naturalist to walk with her on her errand.

A warm spring day and Cari, twelve, was walking with the old kidnapped professor along a dirt road. Flowers were blooming on the ditch banks and bees were busy working the blossoms. They were going to the nursing station to pick up the captive's insulin, provided by his family with a big fee to FARC. They had to walk through a burned village, site of a recent massacre. It had been a village partial to the paramilitary. They were not looking into the huts because of what they might see. A buzzard flapped and scratched, making a lot of racket taking off from a tin roof. At one house, the occupants had tried to pull their stuff out into the yard. A mosquito net was tangled in the bushes. The old naturalist looked at it for a moment, and at the flowers along the road, and he pulled the net down and folded it.

"I think we could take this, don't you?" he said to Cari. She carried it when he became fatigued.

In the afternoon, after Cari gave him his injection, the old man had to teach Darwin to a class of young recruits. The lecture covered principles of evolution that could be stretched to confirm communism as part of the natural order. A monitor sat in on the class to be sure the professor's true opinion did not show through.

They were free then until Cari had to go cook the troop's evening meal, a capybara for Lent. FARC had to allow a little religion, and capybaras do not count as meat during Lent since the Vatican ruled the rodent is a fish.

"I want to show you something," the professor said. "Let's cut this mosquito net in two. We have hats with a brim all round, get them please, and come with me."

The old man took his time going through the woods behind his hut.

On the slope of a hill near a stream was a beehive. It filled half a hollow tree trunk. Cari and the professor put the nets over their hats and buttoned their sleeves. With strips of rag they tied their pants cuffs.

"If the bees get too stirred up we can come another time and smoke them," the professor said. He had kept bees as a hobby before the kidnapping interrupted his life.

The bees were busy. Cari and her teacher stood close enough to the hive, but not too close.

"Their duties change with their age," the professor said. "They are all female, the workers. They start by cleaning out the cell where they hatched. Then they clean and maintain the hive, then they receive nectar and pollen from the bees who go to the flowers, and last they go out to forage until they wear out. Some of these forager bees are new to it. It's a strange new job to them—see, some of them are just circling the entrance, memorizing it so they can find it again. See the little stage at the entrance where the loaded bees arrive back at the hive from foraging? There are the foraging bees coming back from the fields. See the receiving committee stroking them? If a new forager comes back with even a little bit of pollen or a little bit of nectar they praise her extravagantly. Why?"

"So she will want to do it again," Cari said.

"Yes," he said. "So she will work herself to death hauling supplies to the hive. She is being cozened." He looked at Cari for a long moment with his clear eyes. "She is being used. She will go out and go out and go out until she falls and dies somewhere under a flower, her wings worn down to little black stubs. The hive will take no notice of her absence. They do not grieve in the hive. When enough foragers die, they will make some more foragers. There is no such thing as a personal life. It is a machine." He watched her, maybe wondering if she would report him. "So is this encampment, Cari, this system. It is a machine. You have a good and inventive mind, Cari. Don't let them cozen you. Don't limit your personal life to just the minutes you can steal in the woods with someone. Use your wings for yourself."

Cari recognized this sort of talk as the most forbidden kind of subversion. Her duty was to report him to the comandante. She would be rewarded— maybe, instead of bathing with the men, the comandante would let her bathe early and alone when her period came, as his girlfriends did. She would be rewarded. She would be cozened. She thought about her friendly reception into the guerrilla group, the affection she was shown, the fellowship. The family feeling she wanted so much.

This was a family that let her drink at parties. It was a family tolerant of sex, if it was cleared with the comandante. It was also the family that told her to kill the ones who didn't respond, or who ran away. They voted on whom to kill among the runaways. Everyone voted yes. Cari, when she was little, put up her hand with the others, voted yes with the others the first time, and never again. She was not sure what was happening. And then she saw it done, saw them shot where they stood in the water.

The word "cozen" stuck in her mind. In Spanish, "engañar." When she became bilingual both words stuck in her mind.

Later in the day, after the bees, the comandante sent for Cari while she was cooking the capybara. His office was in a small house commandeered by FARC. Three women worked in his office. Their office duties were not readily apparent. All sat on cushions they had made.

Cari came to attention in front of his desk. She was not armed so she removed her hat.

"How is the professor?" the comandante said. The comandante was about thirty-five, a determined administrator, hesitant in combat. A Marxist theorist.

He wore the same round steel-framed glasses he had worn as a student.

"Better, Comandante," Cari said. "He has gained a few pounds. Eating green plantains rather than ripe ones has helped with his blood sugar. I look at his test tapes. He breathes better in his sleep."

"Good, we need to keep him healthy. We will wait two weeks more for the next ransom. I suggest he write to his family again. If they don't pay, the letter after that will contain his ears. And, Cari, you will cut them off." The comandante twirled a paper clip on the point of a pencil.

"Now, Cari, Jorge tells me he saw you with the professor in the woods. The old man was wearing a mask or camouflage. You had one on too. Jorge was afraid the professor had talked you into something. He considered bringing you to me at gunpoint. Cari, what were you doing?"

"Comandante, the professor appreciates the courtesy you have extended to him, and he appreciates getting his medicine. He—"

"And he expresses this gratitude wearing a mask in the woods?"

"He was showing me how we can harvest honey. He kept bees in his life before. Those were bee hats he made. It is a survival skill he thought you might allow him to teach, along with Darwin. He said it could be useful to the troop to get nourishment in this way. Honey will last a long time in storage with no refrigeration. He told me that in an emergency you can bind up a wound with honey because it is almost sterile. We already have the mosquito nets. We could smoke the bees with smudges that don't make much smoke. Not enough for an air patrol to see."

The comandante twirled his clip. His several secretaries looked at Cari with disfavor.

"That is interesting, Cari. You should have approached me before you let him put on anything other than his approved clothing."

"Yes, Comandante."

"I have punished you before for lack of seriousness. Now I am going to reward you. What would you like? Would you like to go for the day to the feria?"

"I would like to bathe alone when my period comes, away from the men."

"That is not our policy. That is sexism. We are all equal in this fight."

"I thought maybe I could bathe early as these fighters here in your office do," Cari said.

Years later on the long road north she would see cozening at the bus stations when the wolves cruised by offering food and feigned affection in exchange for whatever sex the kid could manage or could be shown how to do. Often the wolf had the food and candy in the car and the occasional teddy bear. They did not have to give the child the teddy bear, just let them hold it until the wolf snatched it back and pushed the child out of the car at the bus station. Sometimes the children could keep some new flip-flops with sequins and flowers on them.

Finally the old naturalist's relatives made the balloon payment and he was released. His FARC keepers let him shave and put on the dress shirt in which he had been taken, now threadbare, and his suspenders. Cari looked the old man in the face and asked him if he could take her with him, and he asked his captors. They said no. He asked if he could send money for her release. They said maybe. The money never came. Or maybe it did. Cari was not released.

She escaped when she was fifteen. She escaped with a boy a year older. He had reddish hair and was missing a corner from one of his front teeth. They slept together in the woods whenever they could and he was dear to her. After the first time, sleeping together on a balsam bed on the forest floor, he looked at her like she was holy.

Shortly after dawn on her last day as a soldier, Cari's unit was ordered to attack a village that supported the ultra-right paramilitary enemy. It was during the time of the sides alternately massacring entire villages, though some newscasters called it only "decimating," not understanding the term.

Often villages were taken over by force, by one side or the other. Then the other side destroyed the village and its residents for harboring the enemy. This raid by FARC was to avenge a massacre by the ultra-right paramilitary three weeks before at a village sympathetic to the guerrillas. The paramilitary had killed everyone in the village: guerrillas, residents, their children, their animals and all.

In this way Cari's family was massacred by the paramilitaries in her second year as a soldier. She did not find out for six months, and when she heard she could not speak aloud for two weeks.

FARC's mission was to do the same thing to the other side, kill the paramilitary troops and kill everyone else in the village that sheltered them, with no exceptions, and burn the dwellings. They took some gunfire from the woods going in. Cari fell behind, stopping to bind a poncho over a guerrilla's sucking chest wound, holding it to keep the young trooper's lung inflated until the medic came. She was shot at twice from the forest and she lay flat beside the wounded man, and fired back across his body. She moved off the red dirt road, moving through the trees parallel to the road.

The troops had passed through by the time she reached the village. They had blown some walls off the schoolhouse and the wind was blowing through the strings of a burning piano, sighing, sighing and whining through the strings in the gusts that blew sheet music across the road.

Many of the houses were burning and there were dead in the streets. She was not fired on. She was determined not to see civilians to shoot. Some movement under a house beside the road. She swung her rifle. It was not a soldier, it was a child far under the house, hiding, lying flat behind a cement block supporting a floor beam. She could not tell if it was a girl or boy, she just saw a dirty face and a mop of hair.

She acted as if she had not seen the child. She did not want to attract attention to it. She stopped and bent over her boot lace.

"Run into the woods!" she said without turning her head toward the house.

The comandante was coming along the road from the rear, arriving last to combat as was his practice. She did not want to be alone with him. He was always trying to stick his finger up her rectum, coming up behind her and trying to slip his hand down the back of her pants. To his credit, he did not order her to let him stick his finger up her rectum; it was purely a social gesture.

She had asked him to stop. She had prayed repeatedly for God to make him stop. This was a regular item in her evening prayers. He did not stop.

She was moving faster to stay well ahead when she heard a shot behind her. The commander was squatting, shooting under the house where the child was hiding. She ran back toward him, yelling, "Es niño, es niño!" Her vision was blurred at the edges, very clear in the center. She was running down a tunnel of blurred green foliage and clear at the center was the comandante.

He threw a phosphorus grenade into the house and flames blossomed. He squatted in the yard with his pistol, aiming under the house. Cari was running, her face was numb. He fired once. His long finger found the trigger again, he squatted low to aim, and she stopped in the road, brought up her rifle and shot Comandante in the back of the head.

She was oddly calm. Smoke was under the house now and she saw the child come out at the back of the house and run into the woods. At the edge of the trees it turned and looked back. The child was really dirty. She saw faces among the trees. A hand waved among the trees.

The comandante was too heavy to drag into the fire. Another soldier might come along any second and see him lying there, shot from behind. Death penalty. She ran to the comandante. One of the lenses of his little round glasses was blown out and the other reflected the sky. To look at his kit you would think he was the most martial man in the world. A fragmentation grenade was snapped to the back of his ammunition pouch. She took it off him.

Cari took his hand and put it under his head. She tucked the grenade under there too. She pulled the pin on the grenade and let the lever fly and ran and ran and ran, flattened herself in the ditch beside the road, kept her mouth open as she was trained to do until after the blast, scrambled up and ran and ran again. The comandante's death removed one item from her prayers.

They ran for it, Cari and her red-haired lover.

They lived a year in the village of Fuente de Bendición, he working in a sawmill and she wrestling pots at a boardinghouse and cooking. They planned to marry. She was sixteen.

At that period, you did not desert from FARC and live. At the end of the year sicarios found them and shot the boy in the street, along with his groomsmen, as they were coming in an old borrowed car to the church where Cari was waiting, holding a jasmine bouquet.

When the sicarios came to kill Cari, the church was empty. She was getting her ripped arms bandaged in the village infirmary and she left out the back.

They waited for her at the funeral home. She did not come. They went to the coffin and shot Cari's dead fiancé several times more and photographed the wounds before they left, having neglected to disfigure his face sufficiently when they killed him.

A week later Cari stood at the door of a great house in Bogotá. A servant answered and sent her to the service entrance. She waited fifteen minutes and her old naturalist in his suspenders came to the door. It took him a moment to recognize her, standing on the steps bandaged and dirty, with blood in her wedding shoes.

"Will you help me?" she said.

"Yes I will," he said at once, and turned off the light above the door. "Come in." In all the time she took care of him as a prisoner, he never hugged her. He hugged her now. Her bandages left blood on the back of his shirt when she hugged him back.

The old man's housekeeper took charge of her and soon she was scrubbed and full of supper and asleep in a clean bed. The shades in the house were down: There was a penalty for helping deserters from FARC. It was death. Cari could not stay in Colombia.

And help her the professor did. She rested a week—it took that long to buy her some makeshift papers, and then he sent her north by bus, days and days and days through Costa Rica, Nicaragua, Honduras, Guatemala, she tying the bandages on her arms with the opposite hand and her teeth.

He gave her enough money for bus tickets in Mexico—she did not have to hop La Bestia, the northbound Mexican train where gangs sell spaces on top of the freight cars, where so many fall, and severed arms and legs dry between the tracks. He gave her a note for a family in Miami. Owing to illness the family had to pass her along, to a family who told her she had to work three years for free. Radio Mambí told her that was a lie, and from there she had to scratch for it.

Ever since that time, Cari always carried with her a little something to eat. Usually she did not eat it until suppertime, if then. She always had a small supply of water with her and a folding knife of legal length that she could open with one hand. Around her neck on a bead chain was the inverted cross of St. Peter, who was crucified upside down. The cross contained a small push dagger.

Now, in her cousin's apartment, she slept in the chair beside the baby, nodding as she had nodded on the bus ride north to the Land of the Free.

Toward midnight her cell phone buzzed. Antonio's cell phone calling again. She looked at the phone, glowing in the baby's room. It was hard not to answer. She let the call go to voicemail. The voice said in a German accent, "Kah-ree. Meet me, I can hell-up you."

Right. Come help me, chingaso, and I will hell-up you.

She rocked the baby and sang softly "Counsel to a Parakeet," a song of her Guna grandmother, promising the parakeet a ripe banana and a life of ease when it is sold to a rich Panamanian.

Nodding off toward dawn, she saw in her dream the tough little house on Snake Creek Canal. The house had stood up to the weather, even with a hole in its roof. It was built on a slab. Calming to see there was no space beneath it where a child could come to harm. In her sleep, in that relief from the day, she smiled to dream the house solid on its slab and the baby alive beside her.

CHAPTER SIXTEEN

The first sunlight burned the mist off Biscayne Bay.

Captain Marco's crab boat, trapline threaded over its turning pulley, worked its way north past the Escobar mansion. The boat crew looked particularly busy as the Miami Beach Police passed in their fast patrol boat. The police returned a wave from Captain Marco and throttled down to spare the fishermen a wake while they were trying to work.

Marco and the three-man crew were sweating in body armor under big overshirts. Passing the Escobar house now. They had to look east into the sun. A flash of reflected light from the dark upper windows of the house.

First Mate Esteban was seated inside the wheelhouse, the muzzle of his rifle resting on a pad on the cabin windowsill. He could see the reflection through his rifle scope.

"I see one upstairs inside the open window. He's just got binoculars in his hand so far, rifle beside his chair," Esteban called to the captain.

The dripping line turning on the big pulley lifted the crab traps from the floor of the bay. Ignacio caught the boxes made of wire and wooden slats and dumped the blue crabs into a large bin in the center of the boat. He stacked the traps on the stern, ready to be rebaited. A slow, steady progression up the trapline, lift and empty and stack.

Two boat-lengths past the Escobar dock, Ignacio opened a trap and froze. "Mierda!"

Captain Marco declutched the lifting line and cut the power.

Ignacio could not make himself put his hand into the trap. He dumped the trap into the bin and Antonio's head tumbled into the pile of lively crabs waving their claws in the air. The head still wore the scuba mask. The face around the mask was much eaten by the crabs trapped with it but behind the glass the face was intact, eyes staring up from the bed of waving claws.

On the seawall Mateo appeared. He pumped his fist at them in a lewd gesture, and grabbed his groin with both hands.

"I can shoot his dick off," Esteban said from the cabin.

"Not yet," Captain Marco said.

At the boatyard Benito looked into the ruined face of his young friend. "Call Cari," he said.

"She shouldn't have to look at this," Captain Marco said.

"She will want to be here," Benito said.

CHAPTER SEVENTEEN

Detective Sergeant Terry Robles (inactive), thirty-six, of Miami-Dade Homicide, pulled into a parking space under the trees at Palmyra Gardens. As he turned off the motor, his phone lit up with a call from the medical examiner's office.

"Terry, this is Holly Bing."

"Hi, Holly."

"Terry, this morning I took a slug out of a floater: white Latin male, twenties. Sent it to IBIS at Quantico. They got a hit. The bullet could be from one of the guns fired at your house. The bullet they dug out of your bedroom wall? It's maybe a nine-point match."

"Who is he?"

"Don't know yet. I called Homicide and they gave me your cell. When are you going back to work?"

"The medics have to clear me. Maybe soon."

"How is Daniela? May I ask?"

"I'm just going in to see her. I'll come to you in an hour."

"I'll be teaching a class, but just come on in. Okay if I introduce you? They'll be disappointed if I don't."

"Oh, hell. Sure. Thank you, Holly."

Robles had Sally the dachshund in the car, Daniela's dog. Sally climbed into his lap and he picked her up and got out of the car to move stiffly to the gate of Palmyra Gardens.

Palmyra is the best assisted-living facility in the Southeast. It is in a group of graceful older buildings under big trees. The handle on the gate opens only from the outside.

Several residents were seated on benches in the garden.

Under an arbor near the hedges a preacher of advanced age addressed a group of pet animals that live on the premises. There were four dogs, a cat, a small goat, a free parrot and several chickens. The preacher held his congregation's interest by frequently handing out treats he carried in his pockets. He tried to place the treats on the animals' tongues in the manner of the sacrament, but more often they were gobbled out of his hand. In the case of the parrot, he held the pumpkin-seed sacrament gingerly in two fingers. The preacher had one elderly human in the group, a gentleman whom he provided with M&M's singly and in twos.

In the preacher's other hand he held a limp leather Bible, gripping the spine to gesture with the book and letting the pages fall back on either side of his hand in the style popularized by Billy Graham.

Sally the dachshund smelled the preacher's treats and, drawn to the congregation, squirmed in Robles's arms as he carried her and a small package into the building.

The director of Palmyra Gardens was in her office. Joanna Sparks, forty, ran a tight ship. Robles thought it would be hard to surprise Joanna. She smiled at Robles. Her small dog jumped down off her lap. Robles put Sally on the floor and the dogs wagged and sniffed.

"Hi, Terry. Daniela's in the middle garden. Terry, you'll see a small bandage on her temple. A little bullet fragment worked out of her skin. It was a jacket fragment, not lead. It's okay. Dr. Freeman looked at it."

"Thank you, Joanna. Is she eating okay?"

"Every bite and dessert too."

When Robles left the office, Joanna Sparks sent a nurse after him.

Robles found his wife on a bench in the middle

garden. A ray of sun through the leaves touched her hair and his heart filled like a sail. Robles had to catch his breath. Showtime.

Daniela was seated beside a man who appeared to be in his nineties, very neat in a seersucker suit and bow tie. Robles put the little dog on the ground and Sally, excited and squealing, ran ahead to Daniela and tried to jump into her lap. Daniela seemed startled, and the old man beside her put out his thin hand to ward off the little dog.

"Here here," he said. "Get down!"

Robles gave Daniela a kiss on the top of her head. A long pink scar ran along her hairline.

"Hello."

"Hey, babe," Robles said. "I brought some of Mrs. Katichis's baklava. And here's Sally. She is really glad to see you!"

"May I introduce my boyfriend?" Daniela said. "This is…"

"Horace," the old gentleman said. He may have been unsure of where he was at the moment, but he had reflexive good manners. "I am Horace."

"Did you say your boyfriend?" Robles said.

"Yes. Horace, this is a very nice friend of mine."

"I'm Terry Robles, Horace. I'm Mrs. Robles's husband."

"Mr. Robles, is it? Very nice to make your acquaintance, Mr. Robles."

"Horace, tell you what, I need to have a private talk with Mrs. Robles. Would you excuse us?"

The nurse was watching. She came to get Horace. Horace was not leaving until Daniela said he should.

"Daniela?"

"It's fine, Horace. We won't be long."

The nurse helped Horace to his feet and they went toward the conservatory. Sally kept jumping up and down in front of Daniela, putting her paws on Daniela's knee. She vaguely warded the little dog off with her hand. Robles picked Sally up and put her on the bench between them.

"What's with Horace?"

"Horace is my gentleman friend. I know you, don't I? I'm sure we are friends."

"Yes, Daniela. We are friends. How are you? Are you happy? Are you sleeping okay?"

"Yes. I'm very happy. Remind me, do you work here?"

"No, Daniela, I'm your husband. I'm glad you're happy. And I love you. This is your dog, Sally. She loves you too."

"Mr....Mr. Thank you for your good wishes, but I'm afraid..." Daniela looked off into the distance.

He knew her face so well. She wanted to be free of him. He had seen the expression before, on social occasions, but it had never been about him.

Robles's eyes were wet. He stood up and bent to

kiss her cheek. She turned her head quickly, as she might at a party to minimize a kiss.

"I think it's time for me to go in," she said. "Good-bye, Mr...."

"Robles," he said, "Terry Robles."

He stood in Joanna's office, the dog under his arm.

"A couple of fragments are working out of her back," Joanna said. "We have her sleeping on a sheepskin. Bloodwork is good. How about you? Therapy, range of movement, how goes it?"

"I'm good. What's with this Horace?"

"Horace is completely harmless. In every way you can think of. We tuck him in his bed at eight thirty. He's been here twenty years. Never inappropriate. She doesn't mean anything, any more than a baby—"

Robles held up his hand. She studied him.

"Terry, she's happy. Her situation isn't bothering her much. You know who's suffering from it? You are. Do we know anything yet? Who—"

He did not hear her for a moment, caught in the instant when Daniela last knew him: *They are in their bed. She is sitting astride him. Car lights glow on the window shade. A burst of automatic fire shatters the window, smashes the bedside lamp and a bullet hits Daniela in the head. She falls forward, bumping heads with Robles as he rolls them off onto the floor. He looks at her bloody face held tight against him. He grabs a pistol from the nightstand. Through the shattered window he sees taillights disappearing. He realizes he has been hit too.*

Joanna was studying his face. "I didn't mean to stir it up," she said.

"No," Robles said. "The sorry little piece of—piece of trash that did this had just finished a six-year stretch in Raiford, where I sent him for assault with a deadly weapon. He gets out, a convicted felon with a history of violence, and he gets his hands on an assault rifle and shoots up my house. It took three days to find him and we never got the gun. Where did he get the gun? Where did the gun go? He's doing life now. I need the person that gave him the gun."

Joanna walked him to the gate.

Under the trees the preacher was addressing the animals gathered before him, and his single human parishioner.

"...men might see that they themselves are beasts," the old preacher said. "For that which befalleth the sons of man befalleth beasts; as the one dieth, so dieth the other; yes, they have all one breath; all are of the dust and all turn to dust again."

Joanna closed the gate behind Terry Robles and Sally in the last orange light of day. The dog, looking back over Robles's shoulder at the spot she last saw Daniela, made one small sound as he carried her to the car.

CHAPTER EIGHTEEN

The reception area at the Miami-Dade County Medical Examiner Building has video so the dead can be identified remotely; the floor is carpeted to cushion a fall if the bereaved should faint at what they see.

The lab behind the double doors is state of the art, with door seals and electronic air scrubbers for the smells, and sufficient cold storage to accommodate the passengers and crew from the largest airliner. The autopsy tables are Kodak gray to enhance photography.

Dr. Holly Bing was teaching a small class of future medical examiners from across the country and Canada. They were gathered around the headless body of a man wearing swim flippers. The subject was in the anatomical position and cooled to thirty-four degrees Fahrenheit.

Dr. Bing wore a lab apron over black, her trousers bloused in jump boots with the airborne lace. She is Asian American, in her thirties. She has a comely face and not a lot of patience.

"You have a white Latin male, physically fit and in his twenties," Dr. Bing said. "He floated up yesterday afternoon beside the topless cheeseburger boat off Haulover Beach. Marine Patrol caught the squeal. The body's fairly fresh but hard used, as you can see. He has an appendectomy scar on the lower right quadrant and a tattoo on his left forearm, USMC globe and anchor with 'Semper Fidelis.' Time of death is recent, maybe two days, but he's been gnawed by crabs and shrimp. What's one thing you want to know determining time of death?" She did not wait for an answer. "Water temperature at Haulover, right? Eighty-four degrees Fahrenheit. Later we'll talk about how to figure degree days underwater. His fingers are missing, as you see. He was about five feet, ten inches tall when he was all there."

"What did they cut his head off with, Dr. Bing?" The question came from a fresh-faced young man standing at the neck end of the body.

"See where the saw buzzed through the center of the third cervical vertebra?" Dr. Bing said. "Tooth pitch is right for a Sawzall, six teeth per inch—the usual thing. Sawzall's gaining in popularity for dismemberments in the U.S., it's a solid number two—ahead of the chainsaw and behind the machete. In this case he was elevated on a table or a counter, or the tailgate of a pickup, head hanging forward. He was dead when they cut his head and fingers off. How would you know that? Look on the lab results—the serotonin and histamine levels are not raised in those wounds. Same with the abdominal punctures, done to keep him from gassing up and floating too soon. See the difference in the finger amputations? One finger was sawed off with the Sawzall, the others pinched off with a lopper in the traditional manner. There's a gunshot wound in the thigh, through and through, and I got a slug that was lodged in the pelvis.

"Cause of death?" Dr. Bing said. "Not beheading. Nope, the cause of death is a thoracic puncture wound, through and through. Entry through the left scapular, skewered the heart, exited just inside the left nipple." Dr. Bing touched the chest beside an oblong exit hole with two small holes beside it. Her nails showed red through her gloves as she pressed the chest beside the blue holes. "Somebody want to tell me what did this? Anybody?"

"Stippling?" a student said.

"No," Dr. Bing said. "I told you it's an exit wound. Detective Robles, what would you say made this hole and these two little holes?"

"An arrow, maybe a crossbow bolt. A fishing arrow."

"Why?"

"Because the arrow went through and through and when the line tightened and pulled the arrow back, the arrow twisted a little and the barbs dug into his chest. Might be an expandable broadhead. Be good to check the dive shops."

"Thank you. Class, this is Detective Sergeant Terry Robles, Miami-Dade Homicide. He has seen this before, along with everything else people do to each other."

"Have you got the arrow?" said the young man at the end of the table.

"No," Holly Bing said, "and what does that tell you about the circumstances?"

When no student answered she looked to Robles.

"They had the time to take it out," Robles said.

"Yes, the killer had time and privacy to pull it out. From the shape of the entrance wound I'd say they did not pull it on through. They probably unscrewed the arrowhead from the shaft and pulled the shaft out of his back. They had some privacy to do that."

Dr. Bing sent the class to the lounge for the break. She and Robles stayed in the laboratory.

"I got DNA to Quantico but it's going to be a few days," Holly Bing said. "Jesus, you can wait a month on a rape kit. The slug's maybe a nine-point match—

a .223 one-to-nine right-hand twist, sixty-six grains, maybe a civilian AR-15. It's a boat tail bullet, maybe subsonic."

"You left the swim fins on him."

"Yes, but I looked under them before the class came in."

Holly took off one flipper. On the sole of the foot was tattooed "GS O+."

"'Grupo sanguíneo,' his blood type," Robles said.

Holly took off the other flipper. "I thought you might want to see this before it gets around," she said. On the sole of the foot was a tattoo, a bell suspended from a fishhook.

"Terry, why would he have the tattoo on the bottom of his foot? If it's not visible, it's no protection in jail. Not like a neck tattoo."

"That one is good for bail money from a shark," Robles said. "Or it's good for a lawyer's time, some lawyers. Lawyers that spend a lot of time around the jail. That's a Ten Bells tattoo. Thank you, Holly."

CHAPTER NINETEEN

Nightfall at the boatyard on the Miami River. Leaning palms rustled in the wind. A small freighter passed with tugs fore and aft pulling like terriers to make the turns.

Captain Marco and two of his crewmen stood with old Benito before the open door of the incinerator. A big fire was burning inside it. Firelight and shadow leaped around the dark boatyard. Second Mate Ignacio wore a stained wifebeater.

"Ignacio, put on your shirt," Captain Marco said.

Ignacio pulled a polo shirt over his head. Inside his bicep was the tattoo of a bell hanging from a fishhook. Ignacio kissed a St. Dismas medal on his neck chain.

In the middle of the flames, between big toothy fish skulls, Antonio's head looked out at them. It still wore the scuba mask, eyes staring out as the rubber melted around the glass. The black Gothic cross earring was missing, ripped from his earlobe.

Cari Mora came out of the shadows and stood beside Benito.

She carried a branch of orange jasmine. She stood with the men and looked unblinking into the incinerator. She put the branch of jasmine into the fire to partly screen Antonio's ruined face.

Benito threw accelerant on the fire. Sparks and flames shot out the chimney.

The fire was red on their faces.

Captain Marco's eyes were wet. His voice was steady. "Glorious St. Dismas, patron of penitent thieves, you accompanied Christ in the harrowing of hell. Now see our brother safely to heaven."

Benito closed the incinerator door. It was much darker without the firelight. Cari looked at the beaten earth of the boatyard. It was just like the beaten earth she had seen in another place, before she came to the United States of America.

"Do you need anything?" Marco asked Cari.

"A box of .40 caliber S&Ws would be good," she said.

"You got to do something about that gun," Marco said. "Pitch it."

"No."

"Then trade with me for another one," Marco said. "Benito, could your nephew do the barrel and breechface?"

"Better do the extractor and the firing pin too," Benito said. He held his hand out for the gun.

"We'll give it back to you, Cari," Marco said. "Cari, you need to cooperate, you know. I am jefe here."

Jefe, like Antonio was jefe. I should have covered him from under the dock.

Marco was still talking to her. "Were your prints on the brass—did you load the clip?"

"No."

"You left the brass at the scene."

"Yes." She handed the gun to Benito.

"Thank you, Cari." Marco got her another Sig Sauer from the boatyard office and a box of cartridges. The gun was a .357. That was okay.

Marco spoke close to her ear.

"Cari, do you want to work with us?"

Cari shook her head. "You won't see me anymore."

From the darkness, a signal whistle. Captain Marco and the others were alert to it.

Detective Sergeant Terry Robles got out of his car. He could see the sparks from the incinerator rising above the boatyard. He walked into the boatyard between high stacks of crab traps. A high-pitched whistle on the wind, and the bloodred dot of a laser sight appeared on the front of his shirt. Robles stopped. He held up his ID wallet, open with the badge showing.

A voice from the darkness: "Alto! Stop."

"Terry Robles, Miami PD. Take the laser off me. Take it off now."

Captain Marco raised his hand and the laser dot moved off Robles's chest and winked on the badge held above his head.

Captain Marco faced Robles in the passage between the stacked traps.

"Don't they make you give back the tin when you're on injured reserve?" Marco said.

"No," Robles said. "It stays with you, like a Ten Bells tattoo."

"Actually I'm glad to see you," Marco said. "No, 'glad' is too strong a word, excuse my English. I am 'not sorry' to see you. Not yet anyway. Do you want a drink?"

"Yes," Robles said.

Under the open shed, Captain Marco poured two shots of rum. They did not bother with the lime.

Only Captain Marco was visible to Robles, but he could sense others out there in the dark. Robles itched a little between his shoulder blades.

"I have a dead body with a Ten Bells tattoo. You probably know who it is," Robles said.

Captain Marco spread his hands. Another freighter slid by on the river with tugs at the bow and stern. The thud of the engines made them raise their voices.

"A young Latin man, twenties," Robles said. "In good shape, wearing swim fins. We don't have his head or his fingers. The tattoo is on the bottom of his foot. And his blood type too, written with the G.S.—grupo sanguíneo—O positive."

"How did he die?"

"An arrow or a crossbow bolt through his heart. He went out fast, if that concerns you. It wasn't an interrogation. He died before his fingers were cut off."

Robles could see nothing in Marco's face.

"One of the slugs in him matches a bullet taken from my house," Robles said.

"Aiiiiii. That."

"That," Robles said.

A moth flew around the bare lightbulb, its shadow crossing both of them.

"I want you to know this," Marco said. "On my mother's soul, we did not know the man who shot at your house. I would not shoot into your home any more than you would shoot into mine. Everyone is very sorry about what happened to your señora."

"A lot of people will shoot into a home. And they shoot young men wearing flippers. Are you missing a kid?"

A thump from inside the incinerator, where Antonio's brain was boiling. A swirl of sparks out the chimney.

"My crew is fine," Captain Marco said.

"I want the shooter on the kid and I want the gun and I want the place the gun came from. You and I are okay now. If I find out you know and didn't tell me, we won't be okay."

"You know I have been legit for a long time. But I saw someone important at a family gathering, a First Communion in Cartagena a month ago."

"Don Ernesto."

"We will say an important person."

"Does he know where the gun came from?"

"No, and he wants to say it to your face. If this person ever came to Miami, would you meet him face-to-face?" Marco said.

"Face-to-face. Anytime, anyplace." Robles nodded thanks for his drink and walked away down the dark path between the piles of traps and crates. The laser dot trailed over the ground behind him.

"That will be about next Tuesday, I think," Marco said to himself.

A puff from the incinerator. Antonio's head blew

up and a smoke ring glittering with sparks rose from the chimney like a dark halo.

Marco hoped the police would not identify Antonio soon because the cops would then start working Antonio's pool customer route.

CHAPTER TWENTY

On the third day of Antonio's absence from work, and with his truck unaccounted for, the pool service company reported Antonio missing. A BOLO alert issued on his truck had been in effect only two hours when the truck was found at the strip mall.

A fellow worker, holding an ice pack against her throat, looked at the medical examiner's video and identified Antonio's tattoos.

When Hans-Peter Schneider saw Antonio's identity on the news he knew time was short. The police would be working Antonio's customer list.

Hans-Peter had watched and waited for two days. He spent the time replacing the men he had lost. He had lost two men, not counting Felix. He had only Mateo left.

Hans-Peter preferred an ethnic and language mix in his crews. He believed this made it more unlikely that the crew would scheme against him.

At a whorehouse and novelty store off Interstate 95 he looked up Finn Carter, a burglar handy with tools who had worked for him before. Finn Carter jumped a little when he saw Hans-Peter, but Finn was fresh off serving a nickel at Union Correctional, Raiford, and open to any proposition. The other was Flaco Nuñez, a body-and-fender man and chop-shop operator from Immokalee with two convictions for domestic violence. Flaco used to be a bouncer at Hans-Peter's bars before the health department shut them down.

When the police did not come to the Escobar house, Hans-Peter went back to work.

Carter was grinding along with Flaco.

Hans-Peter Schneider watched from the basement stairs. He was wearing Antonio's black Gothic cross earring, and thought it gave him a certain dash.

He said nothing to his new employees about the possibility of explosives. Jesús could be lying, who knew?

It is not possible to have a subterranean basement in Miami Beach, as the water table is too high. A true basement would either fill with water or float your house. To stay above tidal surges in a hurricane, the Escobar house was elevated on pilings, as was the patio, and the whole surrounded by added dirt. So its basement room, though surrounded by earth, was high enough not to flood except in the king tides.

Carter and Flaco had scraped away the cement from the basement wall to reveal the landward face of the steel cube. A vault door was set into the cube and the entire front face was painted with the vivid larger-than-life-size image of Our Lady of Charity, Nuestra Señora de Caridad del Cobre, patroness of Cuba, and of boatmen. There was no dial or keyhole on the vault door, only a small handle that did not turn.

Carter put an eight percent cobalt bit into his heavy electric drill and coated the cutting tip with black oxide. To get 220 volts they had to run the cord down the stairs from behind the kitchen stove.

Carter crossed himself before he pressed the drill against the breast of the image and squeezed the trigger. Noise and only a small curl of metal.

Hans-Peter considered. He winced at the sound of the drill. His lashless eyelids half closed. He heard in his mind the voice of Jesús Villarreal: *The Lady has an explosive temper.*

He had to yell to stop Carter. He went out into the garden to make a telephone call. He waited three minutes for an answer. Hans-Peter heard the gasp of the respirator before the thin voice of Jesús Villarreal in Barranquilla, Colombia, came on the line.

"Jesús, it is time for you to earn the money I have sent you," Schneider said.

"Señor Schneider, it is time for you to send the rest of the money I have earned," Jesús said.

"I have a vault door."

"To which I guided you."

"There is no dial, only a small handle. Should I open it?"

A gasp and a pause and the thin voice came again. "It is locked."

"Should I force it open?"

"Not if you wish to remain in this world."

"Then advise me, my old and good friend Jesús."

"The arrival of funds will stimulate my memory."

"Danger is everywhere and time is short," Schneider said. "You want to provide for your family. I want to protect my men. What threatens one also threatens the other—is your mind clear enough to follow that?"

"My mind is clear enough to count money. This is a simple matter: Pay what you said you would pay and do it now." Jesús had to stop for several breaths and suck oxygen. "Others might be more generous. Meanwhile I would not disturb Nuestra Señora de Caridad del Cobre, my good friend Señor Schneider." The line went dead.

Schneider reached behind the kitchen stove and unplugged the power cord to the big drill. He went down the stairs and told his men, "We have to wait, or take it out in one piece. We have to take it someplace where we can work on it. It's a big block of steel, Carter. We need privacy."

The television news at noon repeated Antonio's identity and put the police tip line number on the screen.

Schneider called Clyde Hopper in Fort Lauderdale. Hopper did marine construction and had a lucrative sideline in destroying historic houses for developers in Miami.

It is notoriously difficult to obtain demolition permits for historic houses in Miami and Miami Beach. A developer might wait weeks or months for a permit to cut down the old oak trees on a property and knock down a historic house.

Clyde Hopper's Hitachi double-front demolition machine could reduce a house to a pile of rubble in a few hours on Sunday when the building inspector was home with the wife and kids.

The machine had a pack of trash bags by the driver's seat for nests and nestlings and all the animal dwellings that come down with a tree.

When the destruction was discovered, the historical society would bleat and the contractor would be fined maybe $125,000—considered a popcorn fart compared to the cost of waiting for a permit, with the bankers perched on the roof like buzzards.

But it was Hopper's barge-mounted fifty-ton winch and crane that Hans-Peter wanted. He mentioned a sum to Clyde Hopper. Then he mentioned a second sum, and a meeting was set.

"We're pulling it out Sunday, in the daytime," Schneider told the men, sweating in the basement in their wifebeaters.

CHAPTER TWENTY-ONE

Barranquilla, Colombia

A taxi nosed its way to the crowded curb in front of Clínica Ángeles de la Misericordia. A vendor with a pushcart argued briefly with the taxi driver over the parking space, but when he saw a nun in the back seat of the cab, the vendor crossed himself and backed away.

In the disinfectant smell of the ground-floor ward a priest partially closed the curtains around a skeletal man and began the Unction of the Sick. A fly rose off a chipped enamel basin and tried to light on the consecrated oil. The priest saw the passing habit of a nursing sister and called to her to shoo for him. She did not respond but went on her way, handing out small candies to children in her path, refusing them the fruit in her brimming basket.

She took the basket into one of the private rooms at the end of the ward.

Jesús Villarreal lay in the bed. He was glad to see a woman, and pulled aside his oxygen mask to show her his smile. "Gracias, Sister," Jesús said in a faint voice. "Is there a card with the basket? An envelope, a DHL?"

The nun smiled, took an envelope from under her wimple and pressed it into his hand. She pointed to heaven. She went to his bedside and moved things around on the bedside stand to put the basket of fruit where he could reach it. She smelled of perfume and cigarette smoke. It amused Jesús to think of a nun smoking on the sly. She patted Jesús's hand and bent her head in prayer. Jesús kissed the St. Dismas medal pinned to his pillow. "Dios se lo pague," he said. The envelope contained a money order for two thousand dollars.

In front of the hospital Don Ernesto's black Range Rover came to a stop. The bodyguard Isidro Gomez climbed out of the front passenger seat and opened the rear door for Don Ernesto.

The driver of the taxi behind them opened the tabloid *La Libertad* and held it up to hide his face.

Inside the ward the patients recognized Don Ernesto at once and called out his name as he passed among them with Gomez.

The nun was leaving, handing out candy. She

peered at Don Ernesto from under the edge of her wimple and smiled at the floor as she passed.

Don Ernesto knocked on the open door of Jesús's room.

"Bienvenido," Jesús whispered through his oxygen mask. He pulled it aside to talk. "I am honored to receive you without being groped."

"You'll be delighted by what I have to say," Don Ernesto said. "Are you ready to hear it?"

Jesús made a small gesture of invitation with his withered hand. "Curiosity is killing me. At least I think that's what it is."

Don Ernesto took some papers and a photo from his pocket. "I can give your wife and son the house in this picture. Lupita showed it to the señora and her sister. Meaning no disrespect, your sister-in-law is extremely critical and outspoken, Jesús."

"You have no idea," Jesús said. "She has never seen me for the man I am."

"Nevertheless, she was much impressed with the house in spite of herself. And your señora is in love with this house. She finds it delightfully nicer than the house of her stern sister. The señora took the deed to a judge. She has a note from the judge verifying the deed. In addition I will provide a sum of money, enough for your wife and son to keep this house forever. The money is already in escrow. Here is the bank's receipt. In return, I want you to tell me everything: what you took to Miami for Pablo and how I can get at it."

"The method is complex."

"Jesús, don't string this out. Schneider has located the cube. You can't sell me its location; I already know. You already sold that to Schneider."

"What I will tell you is that if it is opened wrongly, you will hear the result for miles. I would need assurances—"

"Do you trust your lawyer?"

"Trust my lawyer?" Jesús said. "Of course not. What a question!"

"But you are the caliber of man who can trust his wife," Don Ernesto said. He rapped on the door and Jesús's wife and teenage son came into the room. Jesús's severe-looking sister-in-law came too, stalking in like a heron, and she looked disapprovingly at both men, and at the room, and even at the fruit, which she believed to be waxed.

"I will leave you to talk," Don Ernesto said.

Don Ernesto, attended by Gomez and his driver, smoked most of a cigarillo on the stoop in front of the hospital before Jesús's wife and her sister and the boy came out of the building. Don Ernesto tipped his hat to the ladies. He shook hands with the boy. Gomez helped them into a waiting car.

At the curb the taxi idled, the driver hidden behind

the newspaper. Gomez walked over to the taxi and moved the newspaper with his forefinger to look at the driver. He looked into the back seat, where the nun was sitting. He tipped his hat to her. The driver was listening to a sad bachata song by Monchy and Alexandra. The driver could smell Gomez's aroma, a mixture of good cologne and Tri-flow gun oil. He sat very still until Gomez went away.

Don Ernesto went back into the hospital with Gomez.

In the taxi the nun lit a cigarette and got out a cell phone. "Give me Señor Schneider. Hombre, hurry up!"

A wait of about five beats. The connection was not good. "Hey," she said. "Our friend went back into the hospital. He is with the big-mouth now."

"Thank you, Paloma," Hans-Peter Schneider said. "I have to tell you Karla did not work out. No, keep the money and send me another one. A Russian is fine."

Inside the ward a patient on a crutch plucked at Don Ernesto's sleeve as he passed on the way back to Jesús's room. Gomez would have peeled the man off, but Don Ernesto said, "It's all right."

The man had tears in his eyes and began a mumbled account of his problems. He tried to show Don Ernesto the sore on his back.

"Give him some money," the Don told Gomez.

"Dios se lo pague," the sick man said, and tried to kiss Don Ernesto's hand.

In his room, Jesús was looking at the basket of fruit with little appetite. It took up most of his bedside stand. A little tune came from the basket. The Mexican bugle call "El Degüello." Jesús tried to look in the basket, but his tubes got in the way and some fruit rolled on the floor. Finally, fumbling, he found the cell phone at the bottom of the basket.

"Dígame."

The voice of Hans-Peter Schneider. "Jesús, you had a visitor. Did you tell him something? Did you tell him something you told me in exchange for my money?"

"Nothing, I swear. Send me the rest of the money, not just this pittance, Señor Hans-Pedro. I can save your life and those of your men with what I will tell you."

"It's Hans-Peter, not Hans-Pedro. It is *Señor* Schneider to you, *Patrón* to you. *Su Eminencia* to you. I HAVE PAID. Tell me how to open it."

"You need a diagram, su Eminencia Reverendísima. I have drawn what you need. Include a paid return envelope with the rest of the money and send it DHL. I will wait until day after tomorrow, *su Beatitud*."

One thousand seventy-eight miles away, Schneider's hairless eyelids flew up, and his eyes bugged out in his head.

"Don Ernesto is there with you now, isn't he? You are laughing together. Let me speak with him, hand him the phone," Schneider said. He had a fleck of foam in the corner of his mouth. He was dialing another cell phone.

"No, I am alone, as we all are," Jesús said. "Send me the money, you pinche gilipollas—you PEPA PELONA—or let me know when your balls pass Mars."

The explosion of the telephone blew Jesús's head all over the room, blew the door of the room into the ward. Don Ernesto's hand was on the knob of the door when it blew open and shrapnel cut him over the eye.

Don Ernesto walked into the smoke. The body was still jerking and pulsing blood. A piece of skull had stuck to the ceiling, and now fell on Don Ernesto. He flicked it away. He looked sorrowful but calm. A drop of blood trickled down his cheek like a tear. He searched the nightstand and found nothing.

"Dios se lo pague," he said.

Chapter Twenty-Two

Academia de Baile Alfredo in Barranquilla, Colombia, is on a street of bars and cafés. The entrance bears the image of a couple dancing the tango, though instruction in the tango is not part of the actual curriculum.

The academy is the current headquarters of the Ten Bells school of pickpocketing, theft, and robbery. The school is named for the test of hanging ten bells from the clothing of a practice pickpocket victim to teach stealth. The pockets are sometimes lined with fishhooks or a razor blade as well to increase the difficulty of the dip.

The studio on the second floor has a large open dance floor. At midmorning a pleasant breeze came in the tall windows along with sounds of the street below.

One corner of the dance floor was set up as an air-port food-court café with a cafeteria line, stand-up tables and a condiment table. A dozen people in their teens and early twenties were on the open floor in street clothing. The students were from six different countries in Europe and the Americas.

The instructor was about forty. He wore Pumas and his glasses were on top of his head. He thought of himself as a choreographer, and he looked like one when he wore a shirt over his prison tattoos. His photograph was on the bulletin boards of airport po-lice stations in cities around the world.

Teams were practicing condiment wipes. The in-structor was talking:

"In a condiment wipe you have to set up early and see the mark come into the food court, so you know in which hand he carries the thing you want to take. Say it's a computer in its case in the left hand. Fix on it. Left hand. You must smear the mustard or mayonnaise behind the right shoulder so he can only reach it with his left hand. And, ladies, when you point out the mustard smear to him as he is walking, you must give him the tissues immediately into his free right hand, so he cannot just switch the brief-case from hand to hand before he wipes behind his shoulder. He must set down the burden. He must put it on the floor and turn his head over the smeared shoulder, away from the briefcase. Push some teta on his arm while you are helping him. A wired support bra will help conduct the sensation through a suit coat. At that moment your partner makes the snatch. You would be astounded how many people smear the wrong shoulder or are late with the tissues. And the ones that do it wrong are sitting in a little windowless room at the airport, waiting on a bail bondsman and dying to pee. All right, here we go. Vincent and Carlita, you're up. Places! Okay, let's have the mark. And go!" The director cupped his hand over his mouth and spoke through his nose. "Flight Eighty-Eight to Houston now boarding at Gate Eleven. Connecting service to Laredo, Midland, El Paso."

In his office off the dance floor, Don Ernesto Ibarra could hear the excited voices, the running feet, the yelled misdirections—Carlita pointing in the wrong direction, yelling, "He went that way, I saw it!"

In his capacity as head of the Ten Bells school and its postgraduate criminal activities, Don Ernesto was writing a difficult letter to the late Antonio's parents, and sending them a check. He thought the check, though generous, might be offensive to them. He hoped so. Then the parents could be mad at him while they spent it, and it would spare him verbal commiserations.

A tap on the office door and Don Ernesto's secretary brought in a burner phone. She held it in a napkin and Don Ernesto used the napkin too. "It will ring in about five minutes. It's someone you know," she said.

At the Tour de Rêve in the busy Port-au-Prince Iron Market many old bicycles are for sale cheap. Most were obtained at night in Miami. They all have been overhauled and are guaranteed for at least a month. Proprietor Jean-Christophe had, earlier in the day, locked the big chain securing the display models out front and carried his laptop to the Café Internet, where he sent an email to Barranquilla. It said:

Mi señor, could you send me a number of convenience?

The reply came within minutes. *+57 JK5 1795.*

At Alfredo's Academy of Dance in Barranquilla the phone in Don Ernesto's hand buzzed and vibrated.

"Jean-Christophe here, sir."

"Bonjour, Jean-Christophe! How goes the band?"

"You remember that? We play the Oloffson when we're lucky, on the off nights when Boogaloo is playing out of town."

"When does your DVD drop?"

"Still in the works, thanks for asking, Don Ernesto. We need studio time. Don Ernesto, I'm calling you because the fellow in Miami who ships me bicycles? He received the call of a guttural person from Paraguay. A person without hair. This person wanted some help in our port of Gonaïves."

"What kind of help, Jean-Christophe?"

"Transshipping something very heavy out of Miami. Hush-hush. Needs to transfer from a ship to a trawler at Gonaïves. I thought it might be of interest. Is such a person familiar to you?"

"Yes."

"The little freighter *Jezi Leve* sails in one week from Miami. I've got a pile of bikes coming on it. My bicycle friend is going to call me after a meet on the boat tomorrow night. Should I pitch this phone?"

"That would be best, Jean-Christophe. Tell your friend in Miami he might wear a kerchief around his neck. Bright orange would be good. Would you give my secretary your bank numbers? Thank you, and good luck with the music."

A knock on his office door. It was Don Ernesto's assistant Paolo, a saturnine man in his thirties with a pronounced widow's peak.

Don Ernesto raised his eyebrows to ask a question and felt a twinge from the stitches above his eyebrow. "Paolo, who do we have in South Florida now? Right now, at this moment?"

"A good crew working the jewelry show in Tampa. Victor, Cholo, Paco and Candy."

Don Ernesto examined the documents on his desk.

He tapped against his teeth his note of condolence. "Have Victor and the crew done any wet work?" he asked without looking up.

In a moment Paolo answered. "They are not inexperienced," he said.

At the boatyard in Miami, Captain Marco answered his telephone.

"Hola, Marco."

"Don Ernesto! Buenos, señor."

"Marco, how long has it been since you went to church?"

"I can't remember, Patrón."

"Then it is high time to work on your spiritual life. Go to Mass tomorrow evening. There is a nice place up in Boca. Go to six o'clock Mass. Take your helpers and pray for Antonio. Sit in front where everyone can see you. Photograph yourselves at the church."

"Some of them, I won't say who, can't really take Communion."

"Let them slink out then, or stare at their laps during Communion. Then, when that embarrassment is ended, go to a good restaurant an hour north of Miami. Send a dish back to the kitchen to piss them off, then tip big so they will remember you. And Marco, see what your friend Favorito is doing."

CHAPTER TWENTY-THREE

The station wagon rolled out of Tampa after the morning rush and headed east across Alligator Alley toward Miami.

The woman Candy rode in the back. She was thirty-five and good-looking, with some hard miles showing. The other three were men in their thirties: Victor, Cholo and Paco, all neatly dressed.

The jewelry courier they had been setting up would have to wait.

"We'll catch him in Los Angeles," Victor said.

"Now that we know what he likes," Paco said, watching avidly as Candy applied some lip balm.

Candy gave him a disgusted look and replaced the lip balm carefully in the phone pocket of her purse, so it would not get through the trigger guard of her pistol.

The storage facility in west Miami was a vast building, pale green and windowless.

To Paco, who tried to write songs, it looked like a slaughterhouse. "Storage," he said, "the slaughter-house of dreams."

Candy waited at the wheel of the station wagon while Victor, Paco and Cholo went inside. When the man who met them did not offer his name, Victor said, "I'll call you 'Bud.'"

He showed the man a coin in his palm. Bud led them down a dim corridor lined with doors. The air smelled like sour shoes and old bedding, wadded and stained coverlets. The air of plans miscarried—divorce furniture, a child's car seat. Paco shivered a little.

The storage cubicles had open ceilings covered with heavy wire mesh, like flophouse rooms. Bud stopped in front of a door and looked at Victor until Victor took out two banded stacks of bills.

"Half and half, Bud. Show me something," Victor said, and gave him half the money.

This storage compartment contained a baby grand piano, a portable bar and a locked cabinet of heavier construction. Bud lifted the seat of the piano stool and took a key from between the pages of sheet music.

"Check the corridor," he said to Paco.

"Clear," Paco said.

Bud opened the cabinet and took out two MAC-10 machine pistols, an AK-47 and an AR-15 assault rifle.

"Selective fire, full auto?" Victor said.

Bud gave him the AR-15 with the drop-in sear that made it a machine gun.

"These are guaranteed inocentes, sinpasados—dumb gats—each of them?" Victor said.

"Bet your life."

"No. You bet yours, Bud."

Bud put the guns in an accordion case, along with loaded magazines and suppressors. He put a short shotgun in the case of a bass saxophone.

Victor looked at Paco. "At last an instrument you can play."

In the afternoon they shopped at the Mall of the Americas, and Candy got some color on her hair.

CHAPTER TWENTY-FOUR

Experienced at grief, Cari stayed busy.

The day after they burned Antonio's head she had a job to do with her cousin Julieta, catering the boat tour from the Pelican Harbor Seabird Station to the rookery on Bird Key, a monthly source of income. What to give the crowd on the boat? Finger food that did not drip.

Empanadas, finger sandwiches, chorizo on toothpicks. Avocado halves full of ceviche when the budget permitted. Give them sweet drinks, rum and vodka, and beer.

They had tried small spare ribs but dripping barbecue sauce got the whole boat sticky and they had to scrub it. They could not have an open fire on the boat, but there were grills the marina let them use and they heated empanadas and steamed dumplings in the clinic's sterilizer.

The tour boat was sizable, an open boat with a canvas top and a bathroom booth beside the helm. It had forty life preservers. Bench seats lined the railings.

Thirty people, many of them Miamians with the eternal company to entertain, had signed up for the tour and they got their money's worth. The tour's purpose was to encourage support for the Seabird Station, which exists on contributions. The boat's regular route circled the natural rookery at Bird Key and then, as darkness fell, went a little way up the Miami River between the skyscrapers of the spectacular night skyline. Tonight they would pause for the fireworks at Bayfront Park.

Dr. Lilibet Blanco, veterinarian and director of the Pelican Harbor Seabird Station, was the hostess for the evening. She had come to the U.S. from Cuba, alone, at the age of seven in Operación Pedro Pan.

Dr. Blanco often let Cari help her with the animals. The doctor looked different tonight in her black pantsuit and pearls. Her husband was with her. He owned part of a jai alai fronton.

Dr. Blanco said a few words of welcome as the cruise cast off.

The boat chugged under the Seventy-Ninth Street

Causeway heading south toward Bird Key, a cluster of two overgrown islands, one natural and one land-fill, comprising about four acres. Bird Key is pri-vately owned and there are no state funds to main-tain it.

The birds were coming home—ibises, egrets, pel-icans, ospreys, herons swarming home, the white egrets and ibises brilliant in the sun against the dark-ening eastern sky.

On each cruise the station tried to stage a release, returning a rehabilitated bird to the wild to illustrate the station's mission and drum up contributions. This evening they had an adolescent night heron in a pet carrier on board, draped with a towel to keep the bird in darkness and as calm as possible.

The sizable fledgling had blown out of the nest during Hurricane Irma and dislocated its elbow. Re-hydrated, the joint healed, wings kept in shape in the net flyway at the station, the bird was ready to go.

The captain brought the boat as close to Bird Key as he could in the shallow water.

Cari carried the container to the stern of the boat and steadied it on top of the railing.

A popular TV weatherman, filmed by his crew, gave a short talk about the environment. He stood at the railing, Cari holding the carrier and standing out of the shot. She removed the towel and opened the container. The bird was facing away from the door, and all anyone could see was its tail. The weatherman was not sure what to do.

"Wiggle its tail feathers and it'll turn around," Cari said.

The big juvenile was still fluffy around the body. Feeling its tail wiggled it turned around at once and stuck its head out the door, saw the other night herons circling over Bird Key and took off like a rocket to join them.

Cari's spirit climbed with the night heron, and this relief lasted until she could not tell the bird from the others soaring over the island.

The boat began a circle around the small island rookery before it headed south to the fireworks in the park.

A number of the passengers had field glasses. One of them was talking to the captain and pointing with an empanada.

Cari put down a tray of finger sandwiches and the captain offered her his binoculars.

An osprey on the island was hanging upside down, hanging from a fishing leader, the cord bunched in a tangle around the limb of a tree, a drying fish still hanging from the hook beside the suspended bird. The bird flapped one wing, weakly. Its beak was open, its black tongue sticking out. The great talons groped at the air.

The passengers crowded the rail.

"Look at the claws on that son of a bitch!"

"See, it was stealing a fish from somebody."

"Well, it won't steal any more."

"Can we do something?"

The water was too shallow for the boat to go closer. They were fifty yards from the red mangrove thicket that edged the island, close enough to see the jumble of trash and brush that covered the ground between the trees.

The trash was a mixed blessing for Bird Key. It kept picnickers away from the rookery, but animals sometimes got caught in the debris.

Through the glasses Cari looked at the bird, tied, its fierce eyes looking up, its great talons grabbing at the sky. Birds wheeled overhead. A bright line of ibises started their descent to settle in the trees for the night.

Cari was seized with the sight of the bound bird. Tied. *The children in the water, tied. They could only press the sides of their heads together, their arms bound behind them. They could only press the sides of their heads together when the safeties on the rifles clicked off, before the ragged volley. Shot and floating away, drifting away in the water with a shawl of blood around them.*

"I'll get it," she said to the captain. "If you can stay here, I'll get the bird."

He looked at his watch. "We've got to be there for

the fireworks. Somebody can come from the station in the dinghy."

"Nobody's at the station," Cari said. "It will be tomorrow."

Volunteers sometimes came to the island to untangle birds, but there was no regular schedule. Some would be afraid of the fierce bird.

"Cari, you've got a job to do on the boat."

"You can leave me and pick me up on the way back. Please, Captain. Julieta can handle the food."

He could see in her face that she was going to do it anyway. He did not want to put her in the position of crossing him because that would be the end of her job. Over Cari's shoulder the captain could see Dr. Blanco looking at him. Dr. Blanco gave him a nod.

"Make it as fast as you can," the captain said. "If it's more than twenty minutes I'll call the Marine Patrol to stand by with you."

The water was fairly clear, about four feet deep beside the boat. On the rippled sand bottom grass waved in a gentle current.

The captain opened the boat's small toolbox. "Take what you need."

Cari got some pliers and some friction tape. And there were some thank-God gloves they had in there to work on the motor when it was hot. There was a small first-aid kit, not a lot in it—a roll of bandage gauze, a roll of bandage tape, some Band-Aids, a tube of Neosporin.

She put the tools and first-aid kit in a cooler along with a towel from the beach bag of a passenger. Cari took off her apron and put on a life jacket. She kept her shoes on and jumped backward into the water. It was about seventy-five degrees but it felt cool filling her clothing. Her feet found the bottom, grass tickling her ankles. The boat seemed high beside her, moving up and down.

The captain handed down the cooler, the lid tied on with a cord.

From water level the many-legged mangroves seemed high too, climbing out of the salt water onto the island.

The bottom of Biscayne Bay is grooved with channels like ditches in the bottom worn by the boat traffic, and Cari had to swim across one, pushing the cooler, kicking, glad she was wearing tied sneakers.

Shallow bottom again. She towed the cooler behind her, and then had to lift it, moving sideways to find a way onto the island through the tangled mangroves.

Under the trees now, not sure anymore of the location of the bird. She looked back to the boat and the captain waved her to the south. Not easy. The ground was covered with trash—coolers, gas cans, tangled fishing line, a child's chair, a car seat, cushions caked with salt, a bicycle tire, a single-bed mattress. Much of it was tidal leavings, wrack and jetsam, effluent from the Little River, which emptied into the bay not far away.

As she waded toward the wrack and jetsam it looked like her life, or almost like her life—she did not see any human parts in the debris.

The bird was hanging from a branch about five feet above the ground, feet and legs entangled in a heavy-duty fluorocarbon leader, spinning slowly, upside down, flapping weakly with one wing, talons grabbing at the sky. Its beak was open, its little black tongue protruding from the pale lavender lining of its mouth. The fish was shriveled, its eyes sunken. It had been dead for several days and Cari could smell it as she stood beneath.

She stood as close to the bird as she could without its beak reaching her. She kicked together some leaves and small branches beneath the bird and spread the beach towel over the leaves.

She reached over the bird and with one hand held the leader and wrapped it around two fingers as she tried to cut it beneath the branch with the wire cutter on the pliers. The wire cutter only kinked the strong nylon leader and did not sever it. She whipped out her pocketknife and flicked the blade open with her thumb without looking at it. Her knife was very sharp.

The serrated part of the blade sawed through the leader, and the bird, though it weighed only three pounds, hung heavy in her hand, the weight pulsing as it flapped with one wing, brushing her legs as she lowered it onto the towel and rolled it up loosely in the towel, its talons digging into the cloth.

She heard one shrill peep as she put it into the cooler with the top ajar. Stepping high through the brush, holding the cooler over her head so she could see her footing as she waded through the trash back to the water. Floating the cooler ahead of her in the water now, steadying it upright as she waded.

A stingray, disturbed as it rested on the bottom, flapped away. A pod of porpoises passed and she could hear them breathing over the cries from the boat. Julieta was in the water now, swimming out to meet her, and a German tourist, seeing the young women in the water, took off his pants in a frenzy of helpfulness and jumped in the water in his skivvies to aid them. He was tall enough to set the cooler on the gunwale of the boat.

To scattered applause they put the bird on the bar table.

Dr. Blanco watched them. Cari looked to the veterinarian.

"What will you do now, Cari?" Dr. Blanco said. "Say I wasn't here." She nudged her husband.

"It's really dried out, Doctor," Cari said. "I'd hydrate, immobilize the wing, keep it warm in the dark until we get back to the station."

"Go to it." Dr. Blanco took a seat where she could see.

Feeling in the towel, Cari got a good grip on the bird, its legs between the fingers of one hand, and she and Julieta did a figure-eight wing wrap with bandage gauze to immobilize the injured wing. As the boat headed south Cari intubated the bird with a greased straw from the bar, finding the opening of the esophagus and sliding the straw down.

"Aren't you hurting it?" a passenger asked.

Cari did not answer. Wearing someone else's glasses, she was piping water from her mouth into the straw, the bird's hot fishy breath on her face, the yellow ring in its eye enormous so close to her eye.

They bundled the bird into the carrier they had used for the rehabilitated night heron and covered the door with a bar towel.

"I can't feel sorry for it like you would a puppy or something, I mean—they just kill things," a passenger said.

"Is that a chicken wing you're eating?" Dr. Blanco asked. She sought out Cari, who was wiping down the bar table and fending off her German helper, who was eager to help with the bar too, and anything else she'd let him do to be of assistance.

"Cari, come see me Monday. I've got something

for you," Dr. Blanco said. "My husband says he's paying a bunch of lawyers anyway, let's see what-if-anything—that's the way they talk—let's see what-if-anything they could do about your papers. He says to back up the credible fear on your TPS they'll have to take some pictures of your arms."

When Cari realized the TV crew was filming, she turned her face away from the camera and declined to be interviewed.

Hans-Peter recognized Cari's scarred arms on the evening TV news. He did not see why she would need both of them. Better a charming asymmetry there. He opened his folder and began to sketch.

CHAPTER TWENTY-FIVE

The Haitian freighter *Jezi Leve* lay at a wharf four miles up the Miami River. The ship's watchman on deck could see the arch of the elevated Tri Rail with its neon rainbow over the river. He had some skin magazines beside him and a short but legal shotgun; the barrel was 18.1 inches long, measured from the breechface. He had an orange kerchief tied around his neck. He was a thorough man and in preparation for his task he had eaten two entire avocados for lunch.

Hans-Peter's man Flaco was beside the watchman, armed with an AR-15 and a pistol in his belt.

As evening fell they watched the lights come on up and down the river.

Flaco could hear faint strains of music from the restaurants downstream. They were playing Nicky

Jam's "Travesuras," there must be dancing, the girls' boobs hopping to the clave, one then the other. That's what they were playing at Club Chica when he danced with the girl with a bluebird tattooed on her breast and they went out to the car and did a couple of key bumps and got to smooching and— whoa! Flaco wished he were having dinner with a hot somebody at a restaurant by the water instead of sitting here with this son-of-a-bitch watchman farting every few minutes.

Belowdecks in the shabby wardroom of the *Jezi Leve*, Hans-Peter Schneider talked with Clyde Hopper from Fort Lauderdale and the ship's second officer, a young Haitian man with epaulets on his shirt. The second officer called in Tommy the Bosun, in charge of the lifting tackle on the ship. Tommy liked to be called Tommy the Bosun because of the pun in Jamaican patois. It meant "Tommy the Hard-On."

The captain was ashore, conveniently blameless. Hans-Peter's man Mateo stood at the bottom of the companionway with a twelve-gauge shotgun.

"Where's Felix?" Hopper wanted to know.

"His kid's having his tonsils removed," Schneider said. "The wife wanted him to be with her at the hospital."

Schneider had the construction blueprints for the Escobar patio spread on the table, along with pictures of the hole beneath the seawall recovered from Antonio's camera.

Hopper had pictures of his equipment. "Here's the high-reach demolition bucket with a hydraulic shear attachment on the barge. We don't have to turn it around to use the crane. We have a fifty-ton hydraulic winch. We'll get it out."

"On one tide."

"We'll do it all on one tide. You sure you don't want us just to swing it into a boat?"

"I want you to do exactly what I said. Put it on the small barge. Wrap it with cargo net. Bring it here."

Schneider turned to the ship's officer. "You will have the lifting tackle ready. Show me where you will put it."

They walked with the bosun back into the hold of the ship.

"In there," the young officer said. "It comes through the main hatchway down into the hold and we cover it with bicycles. On deck we cover the hatch with another pile of bicycles."

Outside on the ship's bridge the watchman saw a lunch truck coming up the river road. Its horn bugled "La Cucaracha."

The watchman held his stomach. He released a cloud of avocado gas. "I gotta drop a deuce," he said. "Back in a few." He left Flaco alone on the bridge with his shattered reveries of romance, waving the air in front of his nose.

Candy drove the lunch truck onto the wharf. She parked and got out.

Candy wore short shorts and a blouse tied at the midriff. She's looking good.

She called up to Flaco on the bridge of the ship, "Hey, I got hot empanadas."

"True that," Flaco said to himself.

"Buck and a half with a cold Presidente. Guys in there? I know they want some. Buck and a half. You could buy me one too."

She waited a beat, shrugged, and started to get back into the truck.

"How do you buy beer from yourself?" Flaco was coming down the gangplank.

"With your money, I hope," Candy said. She could see a pistol print against his shirt. He had left the rifle on the bridge.

She opened the back of the lunch truck. It was half-empty. Two thermos boxes held hot empanadas and cold beer and there was one more large ice chest and a butane grill.

She opened a bottle of Presidente and gave it to Flaco. "Want to sit on the bench? I'll bring the pies." She slung her shoulder bag and gathered the food.

They sat on a bench on the wharf, their backs to the ship.

She patted Flaco on the thigh. "Pretty good, aren't they?"

Flaco was chewing. "Your horn plays 'La Cucaracha,' that's funny," he said with his mouth full. He had difficulty swallowing with his head turned to peer down her blouse.

Behind them Victor, Cholo and Paco slipped up the gangway onto the ship.

"You are very beautiful," Flaco said. "What else are you selling? We could get in the truck."

Candy waited for a boat to pass. She looked up and down the river for more traffic and saw none.

"Give you a key bump first and a hundred after," Flaco said. He showed her a hundred-dollar bill.

Candy pressed the lock button on her ignition key and the lights flashed on the truck.

The ripping sound of two MAC-10s going off in the ship, flashes of light at the portholes.

Candy shot Flaco through her purse, hitting him twice in the ribs. She pressed the gun under his arm and fired twice more.

She looked in his face and saw he was done. She put the hundred in her pocket. Candy threw the bottles and his half-eaten empanada and napkin into the river.

A fish rose to the meat pie. The music from the restaurants came faintly across the water. In the quiet a manatee came up to breathe with its calf.

Inside the freighter, Hopper and the young ship's officer and the bosun were dead. No sign of Mateo.

Hans-Peter Schneider was under the table with blood on his head. Victor shot him again, bullets plucking at Schneider's coat and shirt, dust flying off him. The papers were still on the table. Cholo fumbled for Schneider's wallet.

"Go!" Victor said. "Go! Haul ass!"

Victor and Paco ran for the front companionway up to the deck. Cholo lingered, wanting Schneider's watch. He was tugging at it when Schneider shot him. Schneider got to his feet and ran aft toward the rear companionway. Victor and Paco shot at him, bullets screaming off the metal.

On deck Schneider fell backward over the railing and into the water on the river side of the ship. Victor and Paco shot at him as he submerged. They went down into the hold for Cholo.

Victor put his hand on Cholo's neck. "He's dead. Get his ID."

They ran down the ramp to the wharf and threw the machine pistols into the big ice chest.

Mateo was fleeing in Schneider's car.

"The papers," Candy said. "Where are the papers?" She was dumping her empties in her purse and reloading from a speed strip.

"Papers, shit—let's go," Paco said.

"God damn it. Get the papers. Are you sure Cholo's dead?"

"Fuck you if you think I would leave him," Victor said.

Candy closed the cylinder on her revolver. "Come on."

Back in the hold they stuffed the drawings into Candy's bag. Cholo's dead eyes were drying. They did not look back at him.

On the wharf, Paco ran to the station wagon parked up on the road, Candy and Victor took the lunch truck. They roared away. Sirens sounded in the distance.

The fish beneath the bridge could feel the elevated train approach. The Tri Rail rolled across the river, shaking bugs from the bridge, sprinkling the water with bugs. The waiting fish sucked them down, making swirls in the smooth surface of the river.

Chapter Twenty-Six

Candy drove the lunch truck. She could see the lights of the airport, the beacon sweeping over. She had to speak loudly to Victor beside her as an airplane passed low overhead.

"What does it say on the paper, which garage?"

"Across from D concourse," Victor said. "Right across from international departures. Our flight goes in forty minutes."

They were approaching a level railroad crossing. The crossing lights came on and the warning bell began to clang.

"Mierda," Candy said. She rolled to a stop as a slow freight train crossed the road. Candy turned the rearview mirror to look at her makeup. Her face exploded as a burst of automatic fire swept across the cab from behind. Victor was shot dead beside her.

Candy's body slumped over the wheel, sounding the horn. "La Cucaracha" over and over with the crossing gong and the roar of the train. Her foot slid off the brake and the truck began to creep toward the side of the moving train.

The back door of the truck went up. Bloody Hans-Peter Schneider climbed out of the back, the rags of his shirt half covering his ballistic vest. He carried a machine pistol. Another car was coming, a taxi. The driver tried to turn around and flee but Schneider shot him through the side window and pulled him out onto the ground. He climbed into the driver's seat and fired a short burst into the butane tank in the back of the lunch truck. It went up with a whoosh that rocked the taxi as Schneider drove away.

Schneider dropped the flag on the meter and drove the taxi, its radio muttering. He had shot through an open window, but the passenger-side window had holes in it. He was able to roll the window down. The seat and wheel were sticky and gritty with bone fragments.

The cab probably had no LoJack, but the cab company could see his location by satellite. He wasn't hot yet, but very soon there would be a BOLO out on the cab. He was bloody and wet and his shirt was in shreds. He sang high through his nose as he drove. Now and then he said "Jawohl!"

A bus stop was coming up. An old man sat on the bench. He wore a straw snap-brim hat and a short-sleeved shirt with flowers on it and he held a frosty Corona caguama in a paper bag.

Schneider hid the gun between his leg and the door. He leaned across the passenger seat.

"Hey. Hey you."

The old man finally opened his eyes.

"Hey. I will give you one hundred dollars for that shirt."

"What shirt is that?"

"That shirt, the one you are wearing. Come here."

Schneider held up the money, leaning across to the passenger window. The old man got up and walked to the car. He had a limp. He looked at Schneider with his rheumy eyes.

"I might take two hundred fifty."

Schneider got a fleck of foam in the corner of his mouth. He brought the MAC-10 around to point at the old man.

"Give me the shirt or I blow your fucking brain out!" It occurred to him that he couldn't shoot without ruining the shirt.

"On the other hand, a hundred is fine," the old man said. He peeled off the shirt and passed it in the window. He plucked the hundred-dollar bill out of Schneider's fingers. "I have on some slacks that might interest you—" he said as Schneider drove away. The old man took his seat in only his pants and undershirt and took a long drink from his paper bag.

Schneider drove the taxi to the nearest Metro stop.

Mateo answered Schneider's call.

"I took off in your car," Mateo said. "I'm sorry. I thought you were—you know—like they got you."

Hans-Peter rolled the gun in a floor mat from the cab and held it under his arm while he waited for Mateo to pick him up.

Hans-Peter had two personal rooms adjacent to his online peep-show studio in his warehouse on the bay. One of his rooms had flocked wallpaper and a lot of velour, all burgundy with chinchilla throws.

The other room was the soundproofed tile room with the drain in the center of the floor. It contained his big shower and sauna, with nozzles all up and down, his refrigerator and his cremation machine, his masks, and his obsidian scalpels—both six-millimeter and twelve-millimeter—eighty-four dollars apiece and much sharper than steel.

He sat on the floor in the shower in his clothes and let the hot water beat the blood off of him. When the water ran under his vest he took it off and threw it in the corner of the shower along with the old man's shirt.

There was music in the room. Schneider had the remote in a condom, the receptacle end sticking up like a little blunt antenna. He kept it in the soap dish. He played Schubert's Trout Quintet. It was the music of his parents' house in Paraguay. It used to play all afternoon on Sundays when he was waiting to be punished.

Quietly and then louder, and then louder the music in the tile shower, Schneider sitting on the floor, leaning into the corner while the shower beat the blood out of his clothes. With a quick movement of his arm, his body slack, he raised to his lips his Aztec death whistle and blew and blew and blew with all his breath, over the music, the whistle like ten thousand victims screaming, the music of Montezuma's coronation drowning out the Trout Quintet. He blew until he collapsed, his face near the drain, his eyes open, his vision filled with the circling water around the sucking drain.

CHAPTER TWENTY-SEVEN

Hans-Peter was dry and clean now, lying in his bed, the blood beaten out of the clothes that lay on his shower floor.

Seeking a place for his mind to sleep, he wandered through older and older memory rooms to arrive at last at the walk-in freezer of his youth in Paraguay.

His parents were in the freezer and he could hear their voices through the door. They could not get out because the freezer door was secured with a chain Hans had tied in an excellent chain knot, the way his father had taught him to tie a chain, shaking the knot until the links jammed tight.

Lying in his bed in Miami, Hans-Peter gave voice to the images swarming on the ceiling. The voices of his father and his mother came out of his face, the mixture of their features.

Father: He is kidding, he is going to let us out.
And then I'll beat him until he shits.
Mother, calling through the door: Hans, dear.
The joke is over, we will catch cold and you will
have to wait on us with tissues and tea. Ha-ha.

Hans-Peter's voice muffled now, his hand over his
mouth as he repeated what he heard through the
door, muffled pleadings all through the night, so
long ago.

"*Chug, chug, chug*" Hans went, like the quivering
hose from the car exhaust he taped to the air vent in
the freezer.

When after four nights he opened the freezer door,
his parents were seated and not in each other's arms.
They looked at him, their frozen eyeballs glinting.
When he swung the ax they broke up in chunks.

The chunks stopped bouncing; the figures were
still, like a mural on the ceiling above Hans-Peter's
warm bed in Miami.

He rolled over and slept like an abattoir cat.

Hans-Peter woke in complete darkness. He was
hungry.

He padded to the refrigerator in the dark and
opened the door, appearing suddenly in the dark
room, white and naked in the refrigerator light.

Karla's kidneys were in an ice bath on the bottom

shelf, pink and perfect, perfused with a saline solution and ready for pickup by the organ vendor. Hans-Peter was letting the pair go for $20,000. He could have offered to take Karla home to Ukraine and harvested her kidneys there for about $200,000 had he not been tied up at the Escobar house.

Hans-Peter hated mealtimes and the ceremonies of the table but he was hungry. He wet one end of a kitchen towel and hung it in the handle of the refrigerator. He spread another towel on the floor.

Hans-Peter took a whole roast chicken in his two hands and said the blessing he carried in his heart, the one he was beaten for saying at the family table:

"Fuck this goddamned shit."

Standing at the open refrigerator he bit into the chicken like he would bite an apple, tearing out chunks of flesh and bolting them with jerks of his head. He paused to imitate Cari Mora's cockatoo: "What the fuck, Carmen?" And he bit and bit again. He took milk from the refrigerator, drank some and poured the rest over his head, milk streaming down his legs and running to the drain.

He wiped off his face and head with the towel and walked under the shower, singing:

"Kraut und Rüben haben mich vertrieben; hätt mein' Mutter Fleisch gekocht, so wär'ich länger blieben."

He liked that so much, he sang it again in English:

"Sauerkraut and beets have driven me out; had Mother cooked meat, I'd have lingered about."

Singing, singing, Hans-Peter put into his sterilizer his obsidian scalpels, so popular in Miami cosmetic surgery. He was careful with these delicate blades of volcanic glass. Ten times sharper than a razor, their thirty-angstrom edge can divide individual cells in half without tearing. You can cut yourself and not know it until the blood draws your attention.

From Hans-Peter's mouth came the voice of Cari Mora: "Good chuletas at Publix. Good chuletas at Publix. Good chuletas at Publix."

He wiped his hands on the wet kitchen towel. "There are the lunch trucks," he said in Cari Mora's voice. "I like Comidas Distinguidas best."

And again the bird: "What the fuck, Carmen?"

He picked up his death-scream whistle and blew and blew and blew in the tile room with its floor sloping off to the drain, his liquid cremation machine sloshing end to end like a slow metronome.

Chapter Twenty-Eight

Mr. Imran arrived at Hans-Peter's building shortly after 11 p.m. He was riding in the third seat of a van. A blanket-covered mound was on the floor where the middle seat had been removed. The mound moved slightly after the van came to a stop.

Mr. Imran was shopping for his extremely rich employer, Mr. Gnis of Mauritania, whom Hans-Peter had never seen.

The driver got out and opened the sliding side door for Mr. Imran. The driver was a large, impassive man with a cauliflower ear. Hans-Peter noticed that the driver wore archery arm guards under his sleeves on both arms. Hans-Peter did not get too close to the van. He did not get too close to Mr. Imran either, as he knew Mr. Imran to be a biter, and that he could not always help it.

Hans-Peter kept a Taser in his pocket.

They sat on stools in Hans-Peter's shower room.

"Do you mind if I vape?" Mr. Imran said.

"No, go right ahead."

Some perfumed vapor emerged as Mr. Imran lit up.

The liquid cremation machine rocked gently and gurgled to itself, basting Karla's body with lye solution.

Hans-Peter was wearing her earrings, and a locket containing a picture of Karla's father. He pretended it was his father in the locket, and the locket full of carbon monoxide.

Mr. Imran and Hans-Peter watched the machine for a few minutes without saying anything, like men absorbed in a ball game. Hans-Peter had added a little fluorescent color to the liquid and on the upward motion of the machine Karla appeared, her skull and remaining face glistening.

"That is a particularly becoming shade," Mr. Imran said.

His eyes met Hans-Peter's, each thinking how amusing it would be to dissolve the other alive.

"Did you put her in there alive?" Mr. Imran asked in a confidential tone.

"No, regrettably. She suffered a fatal injury while trying to flee in the middle of the night. Even dead, they do move entertainingly when the heat hits them," Hans-Peter said.

"Could you set up an apparatus like this for Mr. Gnis's den and demonstrate the machine on a conscious subject, do you think?"

"Yes."

"You have something to show me today."

Hans-Peter handed Mr. Imran a large leather folder, the cover tooled in a floral pattern. It contained candid photographs of Cari Mora taken with a telephoto lens as she worked around the Escobar house and garden, along with Hans-Peter's sketched suggestions.

"Um!" Mr. Imran said. "Yes, Mr. Gnis was very enthusiastic about these and thanks you for sending them. Quite remarkable. How did she get the scars?"

"I don't know. She will probably tell you as the work goes forward—I expect there will be work?"

"Oh yes," Mr. Imran said. "I hope I will be privileged to watch and hear that conversation—the conversations are the very best part." He smiled. Mr. Imran's teeth are slanted backward like those of a rat, but their color more resembles the rust orange of a beaver's teeth, with their heavy concentration of iron in the dentin. There were dark stains at the corners of his mouth.

"The major work should be done on the other side, Mr. Imran, because afterward she will be too difficult to move. It's not like simply harvesting a kidney at the airport."

"This is a hands-on project for my Mr. Gnis," Mr. Imran said. "He wants to actively participate in every phase. Does he need to work on his Spanish?"

"It wouldn't hurt. She is completely bilingual. In extremis, though, she will probably revert to Spanish—they often do."

"Mr. Gnis wants the services of Karen Keefe for some portrait tattoos of his mom, Mother Gnis. He would like them drawn on the subject at the sites of the original work when that work is completed and healed over."

"Sadly, Karen is finishing a prison sentence and has about a year to go."

"That could still work into the long arc of the project; Mother Gnis's birthday will come once a year forever. Will Karen be able to travel after her release?"

"Yes, a felony does not disqualify you for a passport if you owe no fines," Hans-Peter said.

"Mr. Gnis values her portrait shading and halftones."

"Karen is superb," Hans-Peter said.

"Would it be useful to provide Ms. Keefe with portrait photos of Mother Gnis to study during her remaining incarceration?"

"I will ask her."

"When can you deliver this Miss…"

"Mora," Hans-Peter said. "Cari Mora is her name. If Mr. Gnis is sending his boat across we could co-ordinate with that. And there may be something else I'd like to send. Small, but heavy."

"She's going to require some gavage," Mr. Imran said. "We could start that on the boat." Mr. Imran made a few notes in his eelskin diary.

The liquid cremation machine began to tinkle in its rocking movement, rocking Karla away.

"It's a chain mail bikini you hear," Hans-Peter said. "It begins to tinkle on the bones as the flesh goes away."

"We'll take one," Mr. Imran said. "Are they difficult to alter in size?"

"Not at all," Hans-Peter said. "Additional snap links come with it at no extra charge."

"May I see the kidneys?"

Hans-Peter got Karla's kidneys from the refrigerator.

Mr. Imran poked the plastic covering them in their slurry of ice and water. "Bit short in the ureters, both of them."

"Mr. Imran, they are going in the pelvis, within an inch of the bladder, not up in the renal position. Nobody's put a kidney up there in years. Get current here. There is plenty of ureter."

Mr. Imran took his leave with the pair of pink kidneys perfused with their saline bath. Considering the recipient could live with one, and with two new incisions would not know the difference, Mr. Imran ate the other one in the car.

His eyebrows went up. "Pré-salé!" he said.

CHAPTER TWENTY-NINE

O ro del Mar is a small fish cannery on the
waterfront in Barranquilla, Colombia. Don
Ernesto's '63 Lincoln with the suicide doors was
parked with the battered trucks of the fishermen.

At a conference table on the top floor, Don
Ernesto was talking with J. B. Clarke of Houston,
Texas, and the plant manager, Señor Valdez. The
Don was helping with a start-up. Two plates of
snails and a bottle of wine were on the table.
Gomez, too large for his chair, sat where he could
see the door, fanning himself with his hat. His
role was bodyguard, but Don Ernesto tolerated his
advice.

Clarke was an ad man. He opened his portfolio.
"You tell me you want advertisements that suggest
exclusivity and prestige. Words like 'prestigiosos.'"

"Caracoles Finos y Prestigiosos," Don Ernesto said. "Would that fit on a label, or is it too long?"

"It will fit. I'm on top of that." Clarke took out drawings of can labels. One of them featured the Eiffel Tower and the legend "Caracoles Finos," another had "Fine Escargots" and a French motif. Another had a chateau in the background and in the extreme foreground a snail on a stem. All the labels said "Packaged in Colombia."

"Why does it say 'packaged in Colombia'? Why not say 'packaged in France'?" Gomez said.

"Because that's against the law," Clarke said. "You're packing them right here, am I right? The French motif is a sales device."

"Yes, that would be unethical, Gomez," Don Ernesto said.

"You could use the Honduran song 'Sopa de Caracol' in commercials," Gomez suggested.

"It isn't French," Clarke said.

"The labels will have animal glue on them. Will we have to lick them?" the plant manager asked.

"No, Señor Valdez. After we test-market we will buy a labeling machine," Don Ernesto said. "You just can them. Show me the shells."

Valdez lifted a box onto the table. He took out a handful of snail shells and put them on the table.

Gomez smelled one and wrinkled his nose. "They

smell of old butter and garlic. The restaurants don't wash them before they throw them out, they just scrape the plates."

"We tried soaking them but the Clorox dims the color," Valdez said.

"Try Fab, with lemon-freshened borax," said Gomez, a bachelor.

Don Ernesto pushed the drawings away. "Señor Clarke, I want you to put something simple and elegant on the label. A candle, a woman's hand on the stem of a wineglass. I want you to convey...you serve these high-class snails to a lady and she will see you for the man you are."

"And maybe she will give you some gatita dulce as soon as she finishes the snails. That means 'pussy,'" Gomez explained.

"He knows what it means," Don Ernesto said. "Now, Valdez, which of these snails are the real French?"

"The green plate."

"Ah, then one plate has the finest French snails, the other is from our own production. You can see the two appear identical. And I believe there is no difference in the dining experience. Shall we try them?" Don Ernesto said.

Everyone appeared apprehensive.

Valdez said, "Permiso, Don Ernesto, if it is possible—"

"That's why we brought Alejandro. Get him, Gomez."

Don Ernesto selected a French snail from the green plate and made a production of eating it as Gomez returned with Alejandro, a man of about thirty-five. Alejandro wore a straw Borsalino hat, an ascot and a flowing pocket square.

Don Ernesto put his shell onto the blue plate. "Alejandro is a man of the world and a distinguished gourmand and food critic. And, Mr. Clarke, Alejandro has friends at all the shelter magazines."

Alejandro took a seat and shook hands with Clarke. "Don Ernesto is very kind. I just enjoy my meals and some people think I'm a grape nut."

Don Ernesto poured him some wine. "Clear your palate, my friend. First, try the escargot native to the south coast of Provence, in France."

Don Ernesto proffered the French snails.

Alejandro worked one around in his mouth. He took a swig of wine and nodded his head vigorously.

Don Ernesto offered an example of his own production.

"And now, those of Brittany, also in France."

Alejandro dug it out of the shell and chewed and chewed. "The flavor is similar, Don Ernesto, but the second batch have more...texture, and the flavor is a bit more insistent."

Gomez was seized with a sneezing fit and had to cover his face with the fat end of his tie.

"Would you buy them?" Don Ernesto said.

"I would actually prefer the first sample, but if I couldn't get that, yes, I'd buy the second one. The second group of snails has been purged in chlorinated water, I think—there is the slight chlorine aftertaste that I find so vexing in city water. You might address that with the Brittany people."

"Would you say the texture is sensual, should we emphasize what you wine experts call 'mouthfeel'?"

"Definitely," Alejandro said. "Mouthfeel, the texture sensual, the flavor insistent."

"Conceptually, that's the direction we are taking," Clarke said. "I'm thinking a lip card for the grocery store shelves. Something like '*C'est si bon—get it on!*'"

"Mr. Clarke, Alejandro, pour yourselves a glass of wine to take with you, and I will meet you at the cars."

Gomez filled his glass. "This wine could be more insistent," he said.

Valdez unlocked the door to the workrooms and locked it again behind him after he and Don Ernesto and Gomez had passed through.

Don Ernesto spoke into his ear. "In Gonaïves I may need to transship something heavy. Your deck tackle will need to lift maybe eight hundred kilos.

You lift it off a boat and put it on a truck. You take it to Cap-Haïtien and put it on an airplane. You will need a forklift at the airport."

"Big airplane."

Don Ernesto nodded. "DC-6A."

"Does it have the good lift at the cargo door?"

"Yes."

"Is the dolly inside or will we need one?"

"It has the dolly. The plane will be loaded with some dishwashers and refrigerators, with a gap among them where my item will go. It is important that it has that exact position in the load. I can give you maybe eight days' notice. It's possible the load may go from airplane to boat instead, depending."

"En su servicio, Don Ernesto. And the papers?"

"Leave customs to me."

Across the back of the room was a production line similar to a poultry processing plant. Dead rats hung by their tails from a moving line. Among the rats was the odd opossum. Women skinned the animals and took filets. A hand-operated stamping machine, ornate and nickel-plated, cut three fake snails from each filet.

"I paid twelve thousand euro for that machine in Paris," Don Ernesto said. "It has been making snails since the time of Escoffier. Another template for stamping cat meat came with it at no extra charge.

Some people think gato approximates snail even better than these organic rodents do."

Don Ernesto picked up a clipboard and checked something off.

Gomez was singing to the tune of a famous soup jingle:

"Gato to gatita, yum yum yum!"

As they left the building, Gomez handed Don Ernesto a black tie and a mourning armband. "Easier to put on here than in the car," he said.

They left the Lincoln at the cannery and traveled in an armored SUV driven by Paolo. They were going to the funeral of Jesús Villarreal.

In the car Don Ernesto took two guarded telephone calls, one from Paco in Medellín. Paco alone had made the airplane in Miami after the shooting on the Miami River, and he had ridden home beside three empty seats.

Was Hans-Peter Schneider dead? Paco did not know. He had seen the bodies of two of Hans-Peter's men and two he thought were ship's crew.

Don Ernesto spoke with him in a quiet voice and then looked out the window for a little while without saying anything. The woman Candy. He thought about the times he and Candy made the big bird fly, breathing hard in a pretty hotel on the island of San Andrés.

*   *   *

Don Ernesto arrived at the cemetery a half hour early and watched from the blacked-out SUV as Jesús Villarreal's funeral procession arrived. Don Ernesto unfolded the note he had received from the widow of Jesús Villarreal and read it again:

Estimado señor,

Jesús would be honored if you could attend his service. It might be as much of a comfort to you as you have been to us, his family.

The widow and her son arrived in a Chrysler, accompanied by a handsome middle-aged man with a distinguished gray coif.

Gomez swept the groups with his binoculars.

"The man in the black jacket is packing," Gomez said. "Pocket holster in the right front of his pants. Wait until he turns around. Shoulder holster on the right side. He's left-handed. Chauffeur is standing by the trunk of the car. He's got a sidearm and the car clicker in his hand. Probably a long gun in the trunk. He's wearing a vest under that chauffeur coat. We've got Ognisanti, and Cuevas behind them. Patrón, why don't I go greet the widow and take her a note from you?"

"No, Gomez. Paolo, who is the fellow with the hair?"

"He's a shitpoke lawyer, Diego Riva from Barranquilla. He defended Holland Viera when he hijacked the bus," Paolo said.

As they watched, Diego Riva passed a black leather envelope to the widow. She carried it behind her purse. About thirty mourners were gathered at Jesús Villarreal's grave. It was only a hole amid the elaborate marble tombs in the Barranquilla Cemetery—there was a nice marble angel in the cemetery at Cartagena that Don Ernesto planned to offer the Widow Villarreal as soon as he could get the rightful owner's inscription chiseled off.

Señora Villarreal wore severe widow's weeds. Their son stood beside her, solemn in his Confirmation suit.

Don Ernesto approached them. He shook the son's hand first. "You are the man now," Don Ernesto said. "Call on me if you or your mother need anything."

He turned to the señora. "Jesús was an admirable man in many ways. His word was good. I hope someone can say the same for me."

Señora Villarreal raised her veil to look at him. "The house is very comfortable, Don Ernesto. The money is in place. Thank you. Jesús instructed me— when these things were done I must give you this." She handed the black envelope to Don Ernesto. "He said you should read it very carefully before doing anything else," she said.

"Señora, may I ask why Diego Riva had it?" Don Ernesto said.

"He handled matters for Jesús. We were afraid our enemies would take it from us. Diego Riva kept it in his vault for me. Thank you for everything, Don Ernesto. And Don Ernesto? Dios se lo pague."

A Gulfstream IV was waiting at Ernesto Cortissoz International Airport. Twenty minutes after the funeral Don Ernesto and his party were airborne on their way to Miami.

Don Ernesto had the papers of Jesús Villarreal on his tray table. He went through them once very carefully, and then he called Captain Marco in Miami.

"Do you know if Hans-Peter Schneider is dead?"

"I don't know, Patrón. We haven't seen any sign of him. We don't see any movement at the house. No police."

"I'm coming. We'll take the house. I want you to find out what your friend Favorito is doing. You can get in touch with him?"

"Yes, Patrón."

"Have you got the girl, Cari? Would she be useful?"

"Yes, but she says she is out of it, Patrón."

"I see. Tell me what she wants, Marco."

CHAPTER THIRTY

Iliana Spraggs, Specialist Fourth Class in the United States Army, had at last gotten a private room at the Miami VA hospital. She lay in her bed with one leg in a cast elevated on a sling. She was a thick-bodied girl, pale beneath her freckles. Her face was very young, but drawn and weary with her plight. Her leg itched in the cast and the afternoon seemed long. Her parents came from Iowa as often as they could.

She had a stuffed dog, and some get-well cards on the mirror. The helium was long gone from the balloon taped to the wall. It hung down like a wrinkled teat. She also had a cuckoo clock. It did not run and everyone knew it. She thought the clock was probably right—time was not passing at all.

Her fellow patient Favorito, thirty-five, with his

cheerful ruddy face, did not have a private room and made do in a ward, where some Marines had taken roles in the TV soap opera playing soundlessly in the corner and were speaking for the characters, making up lewd dialogue as they went along.

A gunnery sergeant was providing lines for the in- génue on the screen:

"Oh, Raoul," the sergeant squealed, "is that a Vi- enna sausage or is it your wee-wee?!"

Favorito was bored. He rolled his wheelchair to Il- iana's room and introduced himself to Iliana as Dr. Favorito, the cuckoo doctor. He asked permission to examine the clock. He took her clock off the shelf and maneuvered his wheelchair close beside the bed. He set the clock on the meal tray over the bed with the back toward Iliana's face so that she could see the works.

"Just a few questions," he said. "You are the health surrogate for the cuckoo, am I correct?"

"Yes."

"You don't have to show me the paperwork right now, but does the bird have any insurance?"

"I don't think so, no," Iliana said.

"For how long has the cuckoo refused to come out?"

"I noticed it about two weeks ago," Iliana said. "First, it was just reluctant."

"And before that it had been regular, so to speak?"

"Yes, it would come once an hour."

"Wow, that's a lot," he said. "Now, to the best of your recollection, the last few times the bird emerged, did it ever sound hoarse at all, or appear disheveled or fatigued?"

"Never," she said.

"Iliana, I see by your beautiful nails that you have a manicure kit."

She nodded toward the bedside table. Favorito got the small pouch out of the drawer. He took out some tweezers and a metal nail file, and was pleased to find some instant nail glue.

Favorito made some adjustments to the clockwork that resulted in a small ping. "Ah! That is what I was looking for. You just heard the 'sing ping,' if I may use a scientific term. In lesser clocks it would be the 'clang twang.'"

He cupped his hand around his mouth and leaned close to the clock, speaking to the cuckoo. "Excuse me for addressing you from the rear, but you should know that it is almost noon and you have been absent for two weeks. Iliana is worried." He reached in with the tweezers, producing a bong. "That is the 'bong of song,'" he said, turning to Iliana, "or more formally *beatos sono*, a most encouraging sign."

He wound the clock and turned it to face Iliana. Consulting his wristwatch, he set the clock hands to the correct time, then went back and forth from watch to clock, having to advance the clock several times, and appearing puzzled that his watch progressed and the clock did not. Then he discovered to her amusement that he had forgotten to start the pendulum swinging.

Now the minute hand moved from 11:59 to 12:00. Iliana joined him in counting down.

"Five, four, three, two, one."

The cuckoo came out, cuckooed once and retreated, slamming the door behind it. They laughed together. Iliana's face felt stiff, not having laughed in a while.

"But that was only one cuckoo," Iliana said.

"How many do you require for noon?"

"Twelve," she said.

"That seems excessive," Favorito said. "You have to let the cuckoo warm to the task."

A light rap on the door.

"Come in," Iliana said, sorry to be interrupted.

Captain Marco stuck his head in the door.

"Hola, Favorito!"

"Marco! Como anda?" Favorito said.

"Excuse me for interrupting you. Could I have a word? We'll just be a second, Miss. I promise."

"One moment, Marco," Favorito said. He made another small adjustment inside the clock and blew on it.

In the corridor with Marco, Favorito held up a finger for silence as he counted down from five. From inside the room came the sound of twelve consecutive cuckoos. Favorito nodded and turned to Captain Marco. "Now," he said.

"Can you get out of here during the day?" Marco said.

"A couple of hours between treatments, yes."

"I got a clock you could maybe fix for me," Marco said.

CHAPTER THIRTY-ONE

Don Ernesto's limo pulled into a parking lot full of rump-sprung economy cars, a few old pickups and a half-done Impala lowrider with the Aztec god of misconduct, Tlazolteotl, painted on the hood.

Gomez got out and looked around before he opened the door for Don Ernesto. A rooster crowed in the distance.

Don Ernesto told Gomez to stay with the car.

In his tropical suit and Panama hat Don Ernesto mounted the stairs of the housing complex, looking at the apartment numbers.

The door he wanted was open and an oscillating fan just inside the door blocked passage. A quilt dried on the railing. A large white cockatoo was taking the air in a cage beside the quilt.

The rooster crowed again.

"What the fuck, Carmen?" the cockatoo replied.

Cari's voice came loud from a bedroom, calling her cousin. "Julieta, come help me turn your mom."

Julieta came from the kitchen drying her hands. She saw Don Ernesto in the doorway.

"What do you want?" She thought he was too well dressed to be a bill collector.

Don Ernesto took off his hat. "Only to talk to Cari about a job."

Cari called from the bedroom, "Julieta, bring her wash things, please."

"I don't know you," Julieta said to Don Ernesto.

Cari came to the hall door and looked into the living room.

One hand was behind her.

Don Ernesto smiled at her. "Cari, I knew Antonio. I want to talk with you. I have come at a bad time. Please go ahead with what you are doing. I can wait for a few minutes. I saw a picnic table beside the building. Could you join me there when you are ready?"

She nodded, backed out of sight and put down something heavy.

Some kids kicked a soccer ball around the parking lot.

In a strip of grass and trees between the buildings of the project there was a concrete table with a checkerboard painted on its top and a coffee can full of bottle caps to use for checkers. Beside the table was a battered barbecue grill. A crow picking scraps off the grill flew to a nearby tree, muttering angrily as Don Ernesto dusted the seat with his handkerchief and sat down. Don Ernesto stood up again as Cari joined him.

"You are taking care of your aunt?"

"My cousin and I, yes. When we're both working we pay a sitter during the day. Don Ernesto, I know who you are."

"And I know what happened to you in Colombia, and I am very sorry for that," he said. "Cari, I am here as a friend of Antonio and I want to be a friend to you. You worked for years at the house of Pablo. You must know it well, its systems."

"I know it well."

"And you know Hans-Peter Schneider's men by sight?"

"I do."

"And the neighbors are accustomed to seeing you?"

"I know some of them, and the people who work at the houses."

"Service people, they arrive there and they are accustomed to you greeting them?"

"Yes."

"I offer you a job with a big benefit for your aunt.

What is the nicest care facility in Miami? The very best one?"

"Palmyra Gardens," she said.

"I want you to consider what I'm going to say as a present from Antonio and an opportunity for you. I'm offering you a scholarship for your aunt to Palmyra Gardens for as long as she needs it, and I offer you a share in whatever we might recover at the house."

A tough old frangipani in bloom over the table attracted bees to its blossoms. The bees made a faint humming overhead.

Cari missed her dead father, she missed the old naturalist she had guarded in the forest. She wished for a steady place to lean for counsel. She looked at Don Ernesto, tempted to follow him.

But she did not see her father in Don Ernesto's face, nor did she see the old naturalist. Above her she heard the bees.

"What would I do?" she said.

"Watch out for me, is one thing," Don Ernesto said. "A woman killed Jesús Villarreal with a bomb. The best defense against a woman is a woman. I need your eye to watch my back. I need your knowledge of the house."

The crow waited impatiently, walking up and down the limb. Cari thought Don Ernesto's eyes looked much like the crow's eyes.

It was obvious to Don Ernesto that Cari did not have great papers, that she was probably staying in the U.S. by the skin of her teeth with a Temporary Protected Status. The U.S. president could cancel everyone's TPS at any moment in a fit of pique, if the president knew what a TPS was.

Cari could sell out Don Ernesto and the gold to ICE at any time, in exchange for good papers and a fat reward. She hadn't done it so far... better to have her inside the tent.

Don Ernesto smiled when the crow muttered at him. He thought about what was coming, the long ache of tension, the smell of fear in a closed and dangerous place. *What the fuck, Carmen*, he thought to himself. *She will be useful.*

"Cari, do you want to bring your cockatoo?" he said.

Chapter Thirty-Two

The Escobar house was quiet. The movie mannequins and action figures looked at each other
across the rooms of draped furniture.

Without Cari Mora to adjust them, the automatic blinds, which used to go up in the morning
and come down in the hot afternoon, remained
mostly in the down position, running up and down
at random with their timers awry. They made twilight in the house for most of the day. The sprin-
kler system turned on and off several times in an
hour.

Shortly before daylight a tree rat pushed open the
cabinet under the sink from the inside and, staying
close to the wall, found and ate the spilled seed on
the floor from the absent cockatoo.

At first light Cari Mora got out of a landscape

truck at the front gate and poked in the access code. The gate swung open and Marco drove in with his crew, Ignacio and Esteban along with Benito and Cari.

Gomez was in a second car parked a block away with Don Ernesto.

"Better keep your mouth open a little bit, Gomez, in case there's a loud noise and a pressure wave," Don Ernesto said.

Bobby Joe's truck still stood in the driveway near the front door.

The truck's windows were down and one door was open, as though it was still waiting for Bobby Joe. It had rained in the night and the truck was wet inside.

Cari looked at the truck. Sitting there wet, it was about the same color as Bobby Joe's brains.

They piled out, armed, with their pockets full of doorstops. Standing on each side of the front door, they tried the lock. Locked. Cari had the key. They shoved open the door and covered Cari while she checked the alarm panel. All off. She turned on the motion sensors upstairs.

"Watch the doorways for trip wires," she said.

Esteban held up a pressure can of jock-itch powder.

Cari shook her head. "No beams in here."

They moved around the side of the house, staying low beneath the windows. A side door stood open. The tree rat heard them coming in and disappeared back under the sink, leaving the cabinet door ajar.

They cleared the downstairs, room by room, yelling "Clear!" as each space was found empty.

They heard something upstairs, a voice. They watched the motion sensor lights but nothing was moving upstairs. Cari shut the alarm off and Esteban set up to cover the big staircase. Marco and Cari went up fast, Cari carrying the AK-47 at the low ready, using the sling.

In a small bedroom upstairs they found the marks of a swift departure. Some clothes abandoned, a TV on. A wasp had flown in the open window and now batted against the ceiling.

The only empty bedrooms were the master, where Hans-Peter had slept, and the room Mateo had used. The other rooms held scattered belongings of the dead: a shaving kit, a pair of burglar shoes with a stud finder taped to one toe.

Leaning in the corner of a bedroom was the AR-15 of the late Umberto, who put Antonio's head in the crab trap and tried to drown Cari.

In the pool house Marco found the harness Felix had worn when he went into the hole. The straps were crusted with blood and sand. Marco looked at it for several minutes. Drag marks in blood led to the dock. He sent Esteban to hose the blood out of the pool house.

Marco went to the basement room and stood on the stairs looking at the face of the cube. His instructions were to leave it alone.

The life-size image of the Nuestra Señora de Caridad del Cobre, vivid on the vault door, made the room feel like a chapel. The struggling boatmen were painted on the sea in front of her. A fresh curl of metal hung from a shallow hole drilled in the saint's side. The big drill lay on the floor.

Captain Marco looked at the desperate boatmen in the Virgin's care and crossed himself.

Don Ernesto was waiting in his car. His telephone rang. Antonio's telephone was calling. He looked at his phone for a moment before he answered it.

"So you have the house," Hans-Peter Schneider said. "I can send the brass there in five minutes."

"Unless I do what?" Don Ernesto said.

"Give me one-third, that's very reasonable."

"Have you got a market?"

"Yes."

"Your market will show me cash?"

"Or a wire transfer anywhere you like."

"All right."

"And there's one other thing I want." Hans-Peter whispered his heart's desire.

Don Ernesto closed his eyes, listening.

"I can't do that," he said. "I cannot do that."

"I don't think you understand yourself, Don Ernesto. For two-thirds of twenty-five million dollars, you would do anything."

The phone went dead.

CHAPTER THIRTY-THREE

In the basement of the Escobar house, Favorito in his VA wheelchair sat at a card table studying the scanned copies of the documents and drawings given to Don Ernesto by the widow of Jesús Villarreal. One of them was a labeled sketch of the cube. Favorito had a stethoscope around his neck and a small box of tools. Several photography floodlights lit the life-size image of Nuestra Señora de Caridad del Cobre on the front of the vault.

With Favorito in the small room were Marco and his first mate, Esteban.

There was a stir, hats off and murmured greetings as Don Ernesto appeared on the stairs. He raised his hand in benediction and greeted them all at once. With him were Gomez and Cari.

Cari nodded to Marco and Esteban.

Don Ernesto stood at the table and put his hand on Favorito's shoulder.

"Hola, Patrón," Favorito said. "Is this everything you got from Señora Villarreal? Did Jesús talk specifics to you?"

"I only got the paper after his death, Favorito. Just before I scanned it for you. Here is the original. It's not much better than the scan."

They unrolled the papers on the table.

"In the photos, the cube looks like 340L stainless steel to me, so it's more than five inches thick," Favorito said. He traced his finger over the drawn diagram. "Here's the explosive charge, this I think is a photoelectric cell, probably diffuse so any light will trip it the minute you punch through the box. You don't have to break a beam to set it off."

"Wouldn't a cell take batteries? It's been a long time," Marco said.

Favorito tapped the papers. "Probably we'll find a power source, maybe under the patio lights, charging batteries in the box. Patio's on a timer, right?"

Cari answered from the stairs. "Yes, a timer. The system's on a double twenty-amp circuit breaker in the pantry. The lights are on from seven to eleven. They were only out four days during Hurricane Wilma."

Favorito looked around, a little startled to hear a young woman's voice.

"This is Cari. She is okay," Don Ernesto said.

"Cari," Favorito said. He pointed at the image on the vault door. "Caridad del Cobre, any connection I hope?"

"Not enough," Cari said.

"This looks like a drawing from hearsay," Favorito said. "No details. No wiring diagram. Here's a bad drawing of the art. With some spots marked 'imán.'"

"Imán: magnet," Don Ernesto said.

"I think we have to look at the back side, see if it has a soft spot," Favorito said.

"Could we punch on through from here, go beside the box?" Esteban asked.

"I don't think it's a good idea to shake it until we know more," Favorito said. "To get through the concrete and rebar around the sides would take what?"

"Two days, if we go all night," Esteban said.

"We need to look down there. I'll go," Captain Marco said. Marco felt he had sent Antonio to his death. He was glad to test himself.

Don Ernesto's telephone vibrated. He looked at it and walked outside. He went into the pool house. The blood had been hosed out but Antonio's blood stained the grout. The grout was maroon now. Small ants swarmed on it.

Diego Riva, the lawyer of Jesús Villarreal, was calling on a patch through Don Ernesto's office in Cartagena.

"Don Ernesto," Riva said in his best friendly voice. "It was a pleasure seeing you yesterday, despite the sad circumstances. I tried your office. Are you in Cartagena? We need to talk."

"I'm away on business. How can I help you, Señor Riva?"

"I want to do you a favor, señor. I expect in the near future you will utilize the information Señora Villarreal provided at such peril to herself."

"Yes, I expect so," Don Ernesto said, sticking his tongue into his cheek.

"I have made a disturbing discovery here. I am informed that one of your business competitors, while making a cursory examination of the material, made an alteration in the documents. It could affect your safety, and I am concerned for you. It is vital the material be restored to complete accuracy, for your own safety."

"I appreciate your contacting me so soon," Don Ernesto said. "What is the alteration? I can give you a fax number here, or you can scan it and send it to my telephone."

"I would prefer to meet with you in person," Riva said. "I'll happily come to Cartagena. Don Ernesto, this project has put me in considerable peril, not to mention the problems of dealing with the señora and her sister, who is difficult to say the least. I would hope you would provide me with a gratuity. I think a million dollars would be fair."

"Caramba!" Don Ernesto said. "A million dollars is quite a gratuity, Señor Riva."

"You need this information. Your men's lives depend on it," Riva said. "Many men less honorable than I might consider a reward from the authorities."

"And if I don't pay?"

"When you have time to reflect, months into an uncertain future, when others have profited, hindsight will show you your mistake."

"Señor Riva, would you consider $750,000?"

"I'm afraid my price is firm."

"I'll be in touch with you very soon." Don Ernesto ended the call.

He summoned Gomez and discussed Diego Riva and his phone call. "He warns of the sadness that can come with hindsight," Don Ernesto said.

"Yes, hindsight," Gomez said. "Hindsight."

"If I pay him, Gomez, he will then sell us to ICE after he has our money. I would like to arrange a meeting at Jesús's grave. I'd like for you to help him improve his hindsight. Do you remember in the movie how Dracula turned Renfield's head around backwards?"

"Yes," Gomez said, "but I'd like to review it on On Demand. Is it all right if I employ my uncle to assist me? He's very capable."

"Yes. Go as soon as this is done," Don Ernesto said.

"Sí, Patrón, but your security—"

"I'll keep someone with me."

"Of this group? Señor, if I might recommend, whoever of the men you take, also take the girl. I think she is very capable. I am a good judge of these things. Remember, it was a woman who killed Jesús."

Don Ernesto did not tell Gomez that there might be fatal alterations in the diagrams of the vault. And he never told Favorito and he never told anybody.

If Diego Riva ratted them out it would spoil the market for the gold in Miami, which is usually an easy place to move illicit gold. The feds and the SEC would be watching for it and they would be all over the local smelters. Jesús had said some of the bars were numbered. The gold had to go out of the country to be recast. It could not be moved in the box if the box had motion sensors.

What was the worst that could happen if it blew up? No witnesses, no evidence, a lot of collateral damage up and down the street. He would lose some good people, but outside of that, nothing really serious.

So. They had to open the box here and do it soon. They had to move the gold before Diego decided to inform the police.

Don Ernesto made a call to Haiti. At Port-de-Paix Airport a man in brown overalls answered the telephone. He was cleaning the fuel filters in an airplane sixty years old. He spoke briefly with Don Ernesto and then Don Ernesto ordered five hundred pounds of cut flowers and three washing machines.

CHAPTER THIRTY-FOUR

The big market umbrella over the hole was for cover from patrolling police and Coast Guard helicopters as much as for shade from the sun.

Shortly after daylight Captain Marco emerged from the pool house wearing a new lifting harness. He carried Felix's harness, crusted with blood and dried silt, and dropped it on the tiles around the pool.

Don Ernesto put his hand on Marco's shoulder.

"You don't have to do this yourself. I can bring up a diver."

"I sent Antonio down there. I'll go myself," Marco said.

"Sí, Capitán," Don Ernesto said.

Ignacio came out of the house with a small suitcase and a backpack. He dumped the contents on the ground.

"Dead guys' stuff," he said. "Some grass, mostly seeds and stems, in the suitcase, a Leatherman tool, a jerk-off—" Ignacio remembered Cari behind him "—ah, this magazine here, *Juggs Triple DDD*, and some shaved dice, and—believe this?—a corduroy whip cup to shoot craps. He was not ready for Miami. That thing would get him killed in this town. I'll get rid of it."

"Get rid of the harness too," Marco said.

Marco stepped under the umbrella as a Coast Guard helicopter passed over.

Benito joined him under the canvas. The old man opened the rod case he was carrying.

He handed Marco a diver's bang stick about five feet long.

"In case you need to make some noise," Benito said. "My nephew made this for you." He held a round of ammunition in his palm. It was sealed with wax. "This is a loaded .30-.30 cartridge reversed butt-forward with a .357 cartridge in the neck where the bullet used to be. Like this. I think you want to load it yourself."

Marco tested the safety on the bang stick, then chambered the round in the end of the weapon.

The .357 round would propel the entire .30-30 cartridge case like a long bullet with its own flaming charge into anything Marco jammed it against.

Benito and Marco bumped forearms.

"Let's go," Marco said. "I'm burning up in this thing." He put on a mask with two charcoal filters and a video camera. Marco looked at Favorito, checking the streaming image on his laptop. Thumbs-up. They bumped forearms.

Lowered into the dark cave with the hand winch. Little jerks as he went down. Marco looked around with his flashlight. The air was thick and warm on his cheeks.

"Down a little, down a little." He extended his feet. "Down, down." He touched bottom. The water was waist deep, the surge up and down not more than a foot. Marco shined his light on the cube, on the human skull, on the chandelier of roots coming through the ceiling of the cave. He could feel the surge from the underwater entrance pull at his ankles. He made a rough measurement with the bang stick.

"The piers are far enough apart so we can drag the cube between them if we get the winch on it." He waded forward, snuffling inside his mask, having to bend low, almost submerge to get under some roots. "The gravel barge is sticking out of the water, but it's not in the way." He reached the cube and the skull beside it. In the shallows near the cube was an eighth of a dog.

Marco took a magnet from his pocket. It stuck to the cube.

"Stainless like the other side," he said. "No soft spots here."

"See any seams?" Favorito said, studying the video image on his laptop.

"Neat bead welds. Flawless, just about. TIG welds, same as the front. They did not make this fucking thing down here."

"Tap it," Favorito said.

A sucking sound from the passage under the seawall. A few bubbles came up.

Captain Marco took a small hammer from his belt and tapped the cube. The sound changed a little as he tapped from the center to a corner.

"Same as the front. Maybe five inches thick. I'm going to look around the edge of the collar. You getting a good image?"

"Wipe your lens, please, Marco."

Marco had a cloth in a plastic bag and he wiped the camera first and then his mask. "Hel-lo. There's a spot here, see it?" He put his finger on the cube. "Size of a pencil. That ain't good. Coming out."

Sucking sounds from the underwater hole into the bay.

Marco waded toward the pillar of light coming through the hole above him. He stumbled over something and the top half of Felix bobbed up, all swollen and gnawed, Felix's organs hanging out where he was torn in half.

Marco, in a frenzy to get away, stepped on Felix. Felix's eye popped and the gas gagged Marco even in his mask. The half corpse began to move, was ripped away as Marco raised his bang stick.

A sucking sound from beneath the seawall. Marco moved as fast as he could through the water, line disappearing fast up through the garden hole.

"Pull it! Pull it!" Marco yelled, his voice muffled in the mask.

He was swinging, his feet drawn up, going up toward the light, and beneath him the bubbles came up in the water in a coffin shape. Esteban and Ignacio were straining at the winch, he heard jaws snap below his feet and then he was up in the light.

Captain Marco sat on the ground wheezing and heaving, his wet suit peeled down to his waist. Offered water, he chugged a couple of swallows and heaved it up into the flower bed. Cari brought him cold water to rinse his mouth and a shot of rum.

Don Ernesto touched Marco's head like a bishop bestowing a blessing.

They looked on the laptop at the images from Marco's camera.

"Probably the iron gravel barge sunk in the landfill is what occupied the FBI's metal detectors," Don Ernesto said.

"They probably drilled and hit it a few times," Favorito said.

Don Ernesto pointed to the spaced punctures in Felix's body. "It's a saltwater crocodile. Gomez—do you recall?—didn't Cesár succumb to a saltwater crocodile after he and his partner defaulted on the loan?"

"Yes, he succumbed in Lago Enriquillo under the bridge near his office," Gomez said. Gomez was practicing judicious speech, like that of the Don. "The crocodile carried him away and it seems very likely that it ate him."

"They can't chew," Don Ernesto said. "They maintain a larder under the water so their meals can rot and get soft and palatable. The crocodile took this man away and then it brought him back to ripen."

Favorito pointed to his screen. "It's a good thing we looked at the cube. See this spot Marco found?"

"It's got a mercury switch, you can't move it," Cari said.

"This was a hole, sealed with solder and polished over," Favorito said. "After you seal something up with a charge in it, you can stick a wire into a hole through the side of the box like that to arm a mercury switch. When somebody tries to move the box—boom. It's old-school IRA."

Cari nodded. "An Irishman was teaching us how to make mortars out of Kosan Gas cylinders and he showed us that too. He signed his name to each one of the mortars. It was 'Hugh G. Rection.'"

"Probably an alias," Gomez said, speaking judiciously.

"Could we cut it from the back with a plasma torch?" Don Ernesto said.

Favorito shook his head. "It was me setting it up? I'd have infrared sensors inside just to catch you doing that."

He took a long breath. "We need the person who set this up. To move it we might freeze a mercury switch with liquid nitrogen. But you've got to keep it cold—minus thirty-seven—or POOF. The optical stuff I don't know."

"Pablo wasn't sealing up his money forever. He meant to get to it. So there's a way in. Will you try it?" Don Ernesto said.

"Let me think about it," Favorito said. He looked down at his numb legs. "Sometimes I don't think enough."

"Think for half an hour," Don Ernesto said.

They studied the images on the laptop. Favorito ran his finger along a weld. "Not everybody can weld this stuff. See, it's TIG. Look what he was doing here, look at him here, just walking the cup along the seam. Really nice work. It's a small club, guys can do that. Let's see the building permit for the patio work, that's when they put this thing in."

Favorito put Marco's photos of the cube into a picture-editing app, Photo Plus, and hit the enhance button.

"Oh, yeah, thank you *Marco!*" Low on the side of the cube in the shadow of the flash were three letters written in grease marker. "T-A-B—Thunder Alley Boats. Don Ernesto, I know where to ask, but I will need some dulces."

"Money or llello?" Don Ernesto said.

"Both is better."

Chapter Thirty-Five

The crocodile, pleasantly full, swam south, sub-merging whenever a boat came by. She was a fourteen-foot saltwater crocodile and she spent part of her time in the Everglades eating juvenile Burmese pythons and the odd muskrat and nutria, but she preferred the salt bay of the South Bay Country Club, where she basked on land near the golf course fairway.

There were other crocodiles in the bay near the golf course, a Nile crocodile or two and some alli-gators near the freshwater springs, all enjoying the warm sun on the plates of their armor.

Best of all, pest control at the golf course got rid of the moths and butterflies that tickle a crocodile's tear ducts with their prickly feet in order to drink the tears.

The crocodile dozed and watched the golfers in their Bermuda shorts.

Unfortunately, dogs were not allowed on the golf course. Sometimes neighbors—often nonmembers—sneaked onto the course in the evenings with their pooper-scoopers and plastic bags, letting their little dogs romp along the water's edge.

Crocodiles, unable to chew, must eat large creatures in chunks after they have decomposed and softened. But Chihuahuas can be swallowed whole, as can corgis, Lhasa apsos and shih tzus. They can be eaten fresh without having to soften in a larder, such as the one the crocodile maintained beneath the Escobar house.

Other than Felix, the crocodile had eaten only one human, a drunk who fell off a boat full of drunks and was not missed at the time or ever accounted for or mourned. She had a buzz for perhaps an hour after eating him.

The crocodile did not dwell on eating humans, but with her prodigious memory for food and the locations of food, she did recall how refreshingly free humans were of hair and feathers and tough hide and horns and beaks and hooves. Unlike a pelican, which is more trouble than it is worth.

Dog owners with their shorts and their plump white legs, sneaking along briskly in the gloaming following their pets, were attractive to her and they could not see very well as the light failed. It only called for patience.

The crocodile suffered some small discomfort in the night passing Felix's headlamp, and left it beside the fairway, to the puzzlement of the grounds-keepers.

CHAPTER THIRTY-SIX

Diego Riva was a handsome man who claimed, falsely, to be the grandson of Cesar Romero. He wore the resentful expression of a man whose substance is less than his looks.

He found sharing nearly impossible and it pained him to see others enjoying nice things.

He was particularly resentful of the comfortable house Don Ernesto had provided for the widow of Jesús Villarreal. The house and the funds provided for Señora Villarreal had not passed through the agency of Diego Riva and he had no chance to wet his beak.

A visit to Señora Villarreal after Jesús's death was unprofitable. He pointed out the justice of his receiving a fee and she was unmoved, sitting in her nice surroundings and cosseted by domestic help, while her fierce sister supported her with acid commentary from a seat in the corner.

Back in his office after the visit, Diego Riva sat stewing through most of the afternoon, his neck pulled down into his collar and his eyes going from corner to corner of the room.

He had altered the diagrams and instructions Jesús provided on how to open the vault in Miami, but he was not sure Don Ernesto would pay him to correct them. And if Don Ernesto did not pay and obtain the corrections, there would be a very loud noise in Miami Beach and no one left to pay him anything.

A little research revealed that the biggest whistleblower reward payout by the U.S. government last year was $104 million. Rewards on recovered valuables ran between ten and thirty percent. Making his calculation with a short golf pencil, he found that on $25 million in gold his reward would be, at a minimum, $2.5 million directly into his pocket.

He decided to rat Don Ernesto out.

His call to the Office of the Whistleblower, Securities and Exchange Commission, Washington, D.C., bounced through a few switchboards before it reached the very friendly voice of a woman at the Department of Homeland Security.

She felt around for his resentments, being accustomed to dealing with disgruntled bank employees and sour corporate underlings. She assured Diego Riva that he was doing the right and righteous thing. The terms she used were "correcting a bad situation" and "seeing that justice is served." She referred to informants as "relators."

She was recording her talk with Diego Riva without the statutory warning beeps. The recorder stood beside a small sign on her desk that read WHAM, BAM, QUI TAM!

There is a certain amount of cooperation among the sundry whistleblower programs operated by the IRS, the SEC, the Department of Justice and the Department of Homeland Security. The custom is, whoever answers the cold call from a whistleblower encourages and pumps the caller and the matter is referred to the proper authority later.

The agent assured Diego Riva that, even if he had given information to another agency already, the SEC would pay off for 120 days after the earlier disclosure.

Diego Riva said he would require written confirmation of a reward and that his information would result in the recovery of a lot of explosives as well as gold in the continental United States.

The DHS agent told him that might require a few hours. Diego Riva said he could provide no more information until the paper was in his hand. He sat by his telephone and his fax machine.

An agent reassigned on short notice from Homeland Security's Container Security Initiative in Cartagena watched Riva's house until relieved in the evening by an ICE agent from Bogotá.

Chapter Thirty-Seven

Favorito looked at Nuestra Señora de Caridad del Cobre painted on the vault door, and the image looked back at Favorito in his wheelchair. The boatmen she protected struggled on the painted waves.

Favorito was seated at his card table. On the table were a gauss meter, a volt meter, a half dozen powerful magnets and a stethoscope.

Don Ernesto, Gomez, Marco, Esteban and Cari were watching, Cari and Esteban on the stairs to clear floor space in the small basement room. Don Ernesto had Gomez beside him; Gomez could pick up Favorito, wheelchair and all, and carry him up the stairs in a hurry.

The image of the saint was floodlit, brilliant in the dim basement.

"We know now they did the metalwork at Thunder Alley Boatyard," Favorito said. "The people I talked to said Pablo himself came to see it. They trucked the cube to the construction site here and lowered it with a crane into the ground. It was all solid ground then. Nobody from Thunder Alley saw it wired. Pablo must have brought somebody up from Cali to do it. The city gas is cut off at the street, right?"

"Yes," Cari said. "I shut it off."

Benito called from Miami International Airport where Don Ernesto had sent him to meet the incoming DC-6A and check out the loading equipment on the old airplane; Benito had loaded a lot of DC-6s in his time. The airplane was refueled and ready and the lift was good, he reported.

There was nothing to wait for. Do it or don't.

Favorito tested his magnets. Spread in front of him were the papers and drawing from Jesús Villarreal. Favorito lit a cigarette.

"Do you think you ought to smoke in here?" Gomez said.

"I sure do," Favorito said. "Okay. According to this diagram, the magnets go on the rondels beside the boatmen, there and there. With the third magnet you go to the legend across the bottom of the painting, *YO SOY LA VIRGEN DE CARIDAD DEL COBRE*, see 'virgin' is spelled with an 'E.' You tap on the letters with the magnet and spell out 'A-V-E.'"

Favorito dried his hands on a paper towel. "Don Ernesto, if anyone or everyone wants to leave, now is the time to do it. I will ask you one thing. From now until we are finished in this room, everyone needs to do what I say. I will respectfully ask that this includes you, Don Ernesto."

"A sus ordenes," Don Ernesto said.

Favorito took a deep drag on his cigarette, dropped it to the floor and rocked his wheel over it to put it out. He looked up at the bright painting of Nuestra Señora de Caridad del Cobre and crossed himself.

He touched the boatmen at the bottom of the painting. "We are all in the same boat, brothers," Favorito said.

At that moment, eleven hundred miles away in the office of Diego Riva the phone rang and a document snaked out of the fax.

In the basement of the Escobar house, Favorito in his wheelchair rolled himself close to the painted vault door and set his brakes.

Favorito placed the first magnet on the left-hand rondel. He listened with his stethoscope. He placed the second magnet on the right-hand rondel. A click from inside the vault door. Favorito blinked several times. He could hear his eyelids clicking too.

"Now tap out A-V-E," he said to himself. "Ave,

and when I say ave, *Nuestra Señora*, I'm talking *ave.*" He tapped A. He tapped V.

He found the E and tapped it. A beat of time. A click.

He tried the handle. It did not turn. But faintly in his stethoscope he heard a tick, then louder the ticking, and louder until it was audible throughout the room. Tick and TICK.

"Clear the room," Favorito said. He did not raise his head from the papers. "Go and keep going, go to the street, get low outside the wall."

"We'll carry you out," Don Ernesto said. "Gomez!"

The big man came forward, bent to lift Favorito.

"No! I have your word, señor," Favorito said.

"Clear the room," Don Ernesto said. "Now. Run."

The men walked fast out of the house, ashamed to run in the house but wanting their lives, breaking into a run on the lawn. From the kitchen the bird said "What the fuck, Carmen?" Cari heard it and ran into the kitchen to open the cage.

In the basement Favorito had a magnet in his hand. He moved it up and down the legend. Ticking, ticking, a little faster, a lot louder, his heart and the ticking in awful syncopation. Favorito held the paper up, looking at the drawing and the brilliantly lit painting both at once. The light off the painting shone through the paper, a light spot where the paper was thin from an erasure. The dot just to the left of twelve o'clock in the leafy halo around Caridad's head in the painting was missing from the sketch. He picked up a magnet and reached up from his wheelchair. He could not reach as high as the halo. He locked his wheels and struggled to push up from the wheelchair with one arm. The ticking sounded like thunder, like gunfire, and he looked into the saint's face and cried out.

"CARIDAD!"

Upstairs Cari heard him. She tossed the white bird fluttering onto the couch. She raced down the stairs into the swarm of light and ticking.

Favorito tossed her the magnet.

"The black dot on the halo, twelve o'clock!"

Cari ran to the painting in three long strides, went up high like a slam dunk and planted the magnet smack on the spot above the Virgin.

TICK. Tick. The ticking stopped. The vault door handle turned itself with a clack. Favorito and Cari were gasping. She bent over Favorito and they held each other as well as they could, until their heaving breath turned to laughter.

Chapter Thirty-Eight

For a quarter of a minute the ticking seemed to stop all over the world. Cari and Favorito jumped when the vault ticked one more time, and then they were busy.

Favorito could not reach everything in the vault. Cari helped him and together they removed the brightly colored loops of blasting cord and the drab detonators to the table, leaving the Semtex in the vault where nails were packed in around the explosive for shrapnel.

They did not want to use a cell phone near the vault, so, when the detonators were out and away, Cari left Favorito in the basement and went to give the all-clear, waving with the bird on her fist above her head.

It went quickly then.

Like a fire brigade they passed the Good Delivery bars, the kilo bars, the rough bars from the illegal Inirida mines and the bags of the fat little tola bars, each a little bigger than a Zippo lighter. Inside the van were three top-loader washing machines, heavily braced inside with rebar welded at the boatyard.

Gomez stood behind Favorito in his wheelchair and hoisted him, wheelchair, toolbox and all, and carried him up the stairs.

In minutes the van was rolling toward the airport through a light rain. On the Julia Tuttle Causeway they met and passed a fast-moving convoy going the other way, toward Miami Beach.

CHAPTER THIRTY-NINE

Two ICE vans with six agents each, four FBI agents, and Miami-Dade Tactical Ops, plus the Bomb Disposal Unit with its robot, streamed across the Julia Tuttle Causeway, using sirens to the halfway point, then a single ambulance siren from there onto Miami Beach.

Miami Beach SWAT and a fire truck arrived first at the Escobar house on the bay. The Miami-Dade Marine Patrol came on the water with two boats, no lights, no sirens. SWAT went in from the front and the back of the house at the same time.

A police helicopter was overhead, flapping the frayed old wind sock by the house's helipad.

Programmed to avoid entanglement, the robot was dubious about the narrow staircase but, with some encouragement from its operator, it went down the steps to the basement room. The barrel of the robot's twelve-gauge shotgun was filled with water to interrupt the firing circuit in a bomb. The shotgun shell had an electric cap where the primer used to be.

The robot's camera showed the open vault, its upper shelves empty, kilo packs of Semtex on the bottom shelf. The bomb squad was glad to see through the robot's camera a tangle of bright detonating cord, detached from the explosives and piled on the card table, and beside the cord was a mercury switch, harmless now. This was a courtesy not lost on the bomb squad.

Three heavy magnets and Favorito's tools, wiped down with oil, were in a loose pile under the stairs.

They found no one in the house but the mannequins, the plaster monsters, the toys.

Police from the various agencies milled in the house. When the explosives left in the bomb truck the dread went with them.

The bomb squad gathered around the antique electric chair in the living room and speculated on whether or not you could use it to heat a pizza. Their sergeant, sitting in the electric chair, said it would simmer but not sauté and that's why it was not still at Sing Sing. Everything seemed funny to them when the bomb was gone.

The Marine Patrol closed off the Seventy-Ninth

Street Causeway and the Julia Tuttle Causeway and searched every boat passing beneath.

Terry Robles gathered the weapons at the house, one AK and the AR-15 from the room of the late Umberto. Wearing gloves, he shucked the AR-15 and took out the sear, a small boxlike aluminum structure from the fire control group that permitted the gun to fire full auto. He showed the sear to the Alcohol, Tobacco and Firearms officers at the scene.

An ATF agent looked at it. His eyebrows went up. "New made," the agent said.

Legal drop-in sears for an AR-15 were all made before 1986. A legal, registered sear will cost you $15,000 if you can find a bargain and have a Class 3 license.

A newly made illegal sear will cost you up to $250,000 in fines and twenty years in Coleman federal prison without possibility of parole.

"Do me a favor," Robles said to the ATF agent. "See if you can move this through the lab pretty quick."

In Hans-Peter's room he found a folder, copies of drawings that were terrible to look at.

Two days later Detective Robles would be undercover with the ATF at the windowless self-storage that looked like a slaughterhouse, where both Don Ernesto's crew and Hans-Peter rented guns.

The proprietor told Robles to call him Bud. His

real name, on the warrant in Detective Robles's pocket, was David Vaughn Webber, WM 48, two priors for cocaine possession, and a DUI.

Detective Robles and agents of the ATF found him because his fingerprint was inside the little drop-in sear on Umberto's rifle.

CHAPTER FORTY

At the airport the van pulled close to the old airplane, and with a dolly Don Ernesto's crew rolled the washing machines onto the cargo lift. The machines loaded with gold disappeared into the airplane to take their places in a line of ordinary washing machines going to South America.

Rain on the tarmac. Reflections of the gray sky pocked with rain. An old 707 taxied by and drowned out the talk. When it had passed, Don Ernesto said, "Come with me, Cari. Come work with me. This place is trouble for you."

"Thank you, Don Ernesto, this is my home now."

"I seriously advise you to come."

She shook her head. In the rain her face looked younger than her twenty-five years.

He nodded. "When I sell the gold you'll hear from

me. Find a place to store cash. Get a big safe-deposit box. When you have the money, feed it into your finances a little at a time until you can invest in a business to run it through. I can recommend an accountant when the time comes."

"My aunt?"

"I will take care of that, I promise you."

Hans-Peter Schneider watched the airplane from the shoulder of the road outside the airport fence. His telephone was in his lap. On a piece of paper he had the numbers of air traffic control, the airport precinct headquarters of the Miami-Dade Police, the Transportation Security Administration and ICE.

Don Ernesto jogged to the bathroom. He was dialing his telephone, talking as he went in the door. When he remembered to look under the door of the toilet stall he saw no feet.

Don Ernesto talked while he stood at the urinal.

"She works at the Seabird Station, on the Seventy-Ninth Street Causeway," he said.

Sirens in the distance, maybe a fire, maybe coming for them. Don Ernesto jogged back to the airplane and climbed aboard.

When the bathroom door slammed, Benito on the toilet could put his feet back down on the floor.

In his SUV, Hans-Peter turned off his telephone, put it in his pocket and wadded up his list of phone numbers. He watched the pilots do the walk-around on the old DC-6A, and then he drove away.

The plane rolled and rolled and rolled down the runway, its four propellers clawing at the air, blowing the grass flat beside the runway. Packed full of washing machines and a few dishwashers—only three heavy ones—at last it labored into the sky, wheeling in a long curve out of traffic and headed south over the sea toward Haiti.

Don Ernesto closed his eyes and thought about Candy and good times gone, and he thought about good times coming. Gomez, directed by the crew to a seat behind the airplane's center of gravity, looked at the massage ads in the *New Times*.

The two names that Diego Riva knew were Don Ernesto and Isidro Gomez.

Arrest warrants were duly issued but by then their old airplane was groaning out over the Florida Straits, free and away.

Chapter Forty-One

Two weeks passed and nobody heard anything from Don Ernesto.

Marco bought a phone card and, on a burner phone, called Alfredo's Academy of Dance. He was told that no one named Don Ernest—was it Ernesto or Ernest?—worked there.

A pleasant morning in North Miami Beach at Greynolds Park beside the lake. Couples in rented boats paddled over the still water. Picnickers were under the trees spreading tablecloths and someone played an accordion. Blue smoke drifted over the water from the barbecue grills.

Cari Mora looked at her watch and took a seat on the edge of the dock. She wore a straw garden hat with a bright ribbon.

A flat-bowed skiff approached the dock.

Favorito was paddling in the stern, his wheelchair folded in front of him on the bottom of the boat. Cari had not seen him since they opened the vault. They had spoken once, for fifteen seconds on the telephone.

In the bow of the skiff Iliana Spraggs was paddling too, her leg propped in an inflatable cast. They wore life jackets. Iliana's face was already pink from the sun.

Favorito smiled at Cari.

"Hi," Favorito said. "Tick tock. This is Iliana."

"Tick tock," Cari said. "Hi, Iliana."

Iliana Spraggs would not look at Cari and did not return her greeting.

"Cari, nobody's heard from our friend from the south," Favorito said. "We might not ever hear anything from him. He took off with it, I think."

Favorito handed up a picnic basket. "Look under the sandwiches," he said.

Cari moved the food aside and saw the bright yellow glint underneath.

She looked around. The closest picnickers were back under the trees. She rooted in the basket. In a loose cloth bag were nine fat little tola bars, stamped 3.75 oz.

"Eighteen of these fell into my toolbox," Favorito said. "Nine for you, nine for us." He continued talking, as much for Iliana as for Cari. "If it weren't for you, Cari, if you hadn't come down the basement steps, I would be hamburger. I been blown up before. These nine are worth around forty-four thousand dollars. They're marked Credit Suisse and not numbered. In time they will be easy to sell. Do it slowly, scatter it out, feed the money little by little into whatever you are doing. Make deposits of less than five thousand dollars. Pay your taxes."

"Thank you, Favorito," Cari said. She took out the bag of tolas and put the picnic basket in the boat on top of the folded wheelchair. "Somebody's getting too much sun," she said.

She offered Iliana her garden hat. Iliana made no move to take it.

Cari looked into Iliana's closed face. "Hang on to Favorito. He's a good one." She put the garden hat in the boat on top of the basket.

They paddled away. Cari put the tolas in her carry-all with her schoolbooks and a bag of Vigoro fruit tree fertilizer.

Out of earshot, Iliana said without moving her mouth much, "She's damn fucking good-looking."

"Yes she is. And so are you," Favorito said. A moment passed before Iliana put the hat on and waved to Cari from the boat. Possibly Iliana smiled.

Cari took the bus to work on her house-to-be near the Snake Creek Canal.

Chapter Forty-Two

A warm day near Christmas. The frangipanis had dropped their leaves to face the seventy-five-degree winter. The big leaves blew against Cari Mora's legs as she walked from the bus stop toward her house near the Snake Creek Canal.

She carried two canvas bags. A blooming hot-pink shrimp plant was in one bag and her schoolbooks were in the other, together with a copy of *Span Tables for Joists and Rafters* from the American Wood Council.

Some neighbor children, average age eight, were putting together a Nativity scene in their front yard.

They had figures of Mary and Joseph, the baby Jesus in the manger, along with the animal residents of the stable: a goat, a donkey, a sheep and three turtles.

A pipe tent pole was set in the ground in the center of the scene. Two girls and a boy fastened strings of lights over the pipe and spread them like tent ropes to make a colorful Christmas tree over the manger scene.

Their mother watched from the porch. She had custody of the low-voltage transformer, the cord coiled under her chair.

Cari smiled at the woman on the porch. "That's a nice nacimiento," she said to the children.

"Thank you," the older girl said. "Kmart is the only place you can find a nacimiento of plástico that will stand up to the rain. The plaster ones melt."

"You have turtles here in the stable with Joseph and Mary and the baby Jesus."

"Well, Kmart was out of Wise Men or Kings, and we already had these turtles. They're wood, but we dipped them in Future in case it rains."

"So these turtles are…"

"Claro—these are the Three Wise Turtles," the little boy said. "If we can get some Wise Men or Kings of Orient Are, then the turtles will be like regular turtles who live together here in the stable. Friends with the donkey and the sheep."

"We'll grub them up so they look like the ones in Snake Creek," the girl said.

"Great nacimiento," Cari said. "Thanks for sharing it with me."

"You're welcome. Come see it lit up when Mom plugs it in. Feliz Navidad."

Cari could hear whistling as she approached her house with the blue tarp on the roof. The whistling started as a peep or two and grew louder and faster up and down the street until it might have been a couple of small steam calliopes. She recognized Silbo Gomero whistle talk.

She suspected the whistle talk was about the man sitting on the front steps of her house.

Cari switched the bag with the heavy potted plant to hang from her right hand. It swung loose at her side.

The man stood up when he saw her coming.

Cari stopped at the corner of her yard and inspected a plant that was turning yellow.

She could see her visitor was packing high on the right side of his belt—the butt of the pistol printed against his jacket. Instead of using the walk, she approached across the grass to keep the sun in his eyes.

"Ms. Mora, I'm Detective Terry Robles, Miami-Dade PD. Could you talk with me for a few minutes?" For courtesy's sake he showed her his ID instead of the tin.

She did not go close enough to read the ID. She wondered if he had zip-tie handcuffs on his belt.

Terry Robles saw that Cari's face was the face in

the drawings he carried in a folder under his arm. The drawings felt like dirty and shameful things to him now instead of just evidence; they felt hot and awful under his arm.

Cari did not want Terry Robles in her house, where she rearranged her three pieces of furniture several times a week. He was a cop, like ICE. She did not want him in there.

Cari invited Robles to sit at a table in the garden and not in the house.

On the back porch the cockatoo was responding to the Silbo Gomero whistling from next door. The bird whistled and yelled back in English and in Spanish.

"Do you understand whistle talk?" Robles asked.

"No. My neighbors save cell phone minutes this way. Never get hacked. Please excuse the bird's language, she's always eavesdropping and butting in on their conversations—if she says something to you it's not personal at all."

"Ms. Mora, a lot has happened at the house where you used to work. Do you know any of the people who were staying there?"

"I was only with them for a couple of days," Cari said.

"Who hired you for that couple of days?"

"They said it was a film company, there was a name on the permit. A lot of people shot film there the last couple of years, commercials for TV using the props there in the house."

"Did you know any of this crew?"

"The boss was a tall man they called Hans-Peter."

"Do you know what they found in the house?"

"No. I didn't like those people and I quit the second day."

"Why?"

"They were jailbirds. I didn't like the way they acted."

"Did you register a complaint anywhere?"

"I registered my complaint with them before I left."

Robles nodded. "Some of them are dead, others are missing."

He could see no reaction in Cari.

"You're in school."

"Miami Dade. I just started."

"What do you want to do?"

"I want to be a veterinarian. I'm taking pre-med."

"You recently got your Temporary Protected Status and your work permit extended. Congratulations on that."

"Thank you."

She could see it coming.

Robles shifted in his seat. "You're on the citizenship track. You have a home health license, you've nursed old people, you've cleaned houses. That crew took a lot of gold out of the house where you worked. Ms. Mora, did you get any of it?"

"Gold? I got grocery money from them, and not much of that."

Three tola bars remained in the possum nest in the attic.

"Last year you declared just a modest income to the IRS, but recently you were able to buy this house."

"It's still mostly the bank's house. My cousin's brother-in-law in Quito owns it. I'm taking care of it. Fixing it up."

This was true, on paper. She could show this son of a bitch.

Anger swelled in Cari, looking into Robles's face, into dark eyes like hers in the backyard of her own house.

She did not think it could come here, the trouble. She did not think it would come to her garden, to her house, built on a slab where no child could come to harm underneath.

Robles's face looked clearer to her than the garden around him. Her vision was very clear in the center, as it had been when she saw Comandante in Colombia shooting at the child under the house.

Cari looked up at her own mango tree, listened to it breathe in the wind, and she took a deep breath and another.

A bee, pressed for winter forage, came to the shrimp plant in her bag and poked around in the blossoms. Cari flashed on the old naturalist she had cared for in Colombia, his glasses folded in his pocket, his bee hat on his head.

Her anger at Robles was unreasonable and she knew it.

Cari stood up at the table. "Detective Robles, I'm going to offer you a glass of iced tea and ask you to state your business."

As a young Marine, Terry Robles had been for six surreal weeks the light-heavyweight boxing champion of the Pacific Fleet; he saw something in Cari's face that he recognized.

Okay. Okay. Showtime. "Okay," he said, after hearing "okay" ten times in his head. "Have you got any idea what Hans-Peter Schneider intended to do with you?"

"No."

"Hans-Peter Schneider provides women for the miners in illegal gold mines in Colombia and Peru. A lot of them get mercury poisoning because the mines pollute the water. That makes it hard to sell their organs when they die. He sells human organs that do not have mercury poisoning. He harvests them in motels. He sells mutilated women to specialty clubs in various parts of the world. He does custom modifications on the women. My point is, if he doesn't catch you he'll make some other woman squeal and squeal."

No visible reaction from Cari.

"Here are his sketches of designs for you. Again, I apologize for this, but we have to get serious."

Robles passed a sheaf of drawings over to Cari, facedown.

She turned them over one by one. From the standpoint of craftsmanship, they were very good drawings. In the first one, she was left with only one limb—an arm and hand with which to provide pleasure to her masters—and she was tattooed with portraits of Mother Gnis. There was no vestige left of her other extremities. She was like a stump with a single branchy limb. A little note across the corner said "Boston Butt."

The drawings went downhill from there. She looked at all of them, stacked them back into a sheaf and pushed them across the table to Robles.

"You could help us catch Hans-Peter," he said.

"How?"

"He's obsessed with you. I want him, and Interpol wants him. We need to put his sick and rich customers in prison or an asylum, where they belong. I want Hans-Peter to stop tearing up women for them. You can attract him."

"Do you know where Hans-Peter Schneider is?"

"His credit cards have been used in Bogotá,

Colombia, and in Barranquilla in the last two days, and his telephone has made some calls from Bogotá. But he'll be back. If he doesn't come back, we have to go proactive and travel with Interpol. An informant has identified some of his customers. One has a villa in Sardinia. I can fix your absence for you at school and at your job. Would you do that? Would you go with me to nail him?"

"Yes."

"And next I want to put in prison the men who rented out the guns," Robles said.

Robles had made arrests in the case of the gun rentals, but he needed to show a jury that those same guns were in the hands of the felons.

"One of those guns shot my wife," he said. "And shot me, and shot up my house, which looks a lot like this one. I like my house the same way you like your house—I mean the way you like your cousin's brother-in-law's house. Did Hans-Peter Schneider have guns that you saw?"

"Yes."

"What did you see? Could you describe the guns?"

"Describe the guns?"

"I read your application to extend the TPS. I know your background. Could you say for sure they were not prop movie guns?"

"They had two AKs, selective fire with suppressors, and a couple of AR-15s, one with a bump stock. They had thirty-round banana clips for everything and a drum for one of the AKs. Hans-Peter Schneider, the tall one, carried a Glock nine-millimeter in a Jackass rig behind his back. Do you take lemon?"

"I won't have tea. Ms. Mora, I can't get a twenty-four seven security detail for you at your home, but I can offer you a couple of witness protection facilities where you could stay and nobody can find you. You could stay there just until—"

"No. This is where I live."

"Would you do me a favor and just look at the safe houses?"

"No, Detective, I've seen the ones at Krome."

"Do you carry a cell phone all the time where I can reach you?"

"Yes."

"I'm going to ask the North Miami Beach PD to pass by here a lot."

"All right."

Detective Terry Robles found Cari to be a very pleasant sight on this golden afternoon, even though she did not like him. He had been alone a lot. He thought of his wife at Palmyra with the sun on her hair. He needed to leave this place.

"There's a BOLO out on Hans-Peter," he said. "When we spot him I'll be on the phone to you. Lock up," he said.

"Merry Christmas to you, Detective Robles."

"Feliz Navidad," Robles said.

Well, maybe she doesn't HATE me—not that it makes any difference in the job or anything, Terry Robles thought, walking to his car.

Chapter Forty-Three

Hans-Peter Schneider had everything he needed for the moment: He had half the $200,000 fee he would charge for delivering Cari to Mr. Gnis and supervising her modification. He had the use of his headquarters here in Miami, which was nowhere listed in his name, and his boat, registered to a company in Delaware.

He had Paloma in Colombia working his credit cards and telephone.

He had a note from the imprisoned tattoo artist Karen Keefe agreeing to come to Mauritania upon completion of her sentence to decorate Cari— Hans-Peter had provided the tattoo artist with a drawing of Mother Gnis's face with which to practice.

He equipped himself with a JM Standard CO_2 injection rifle with darts containing enough azaperone to immobilize a 125-pound mammal. He had a nine-millimeter pistol in the back of his waistband.

Hans-Peter had found that it is easier to move a person who is bound if the subject is in a ventilated body bag with carrying straps. Generally, odor- and fluid-proof body bags are airtight and the occupant, if not already dead, will smother. The bag in Hans-Peter's kit was well ventilated and single-layer canvas.

He had heavy-duty zip-tie strips, chloroform and face pads. He had diet supplements for gavage on the boat, and his obsidian scalpels in case they wanted to do a little something on the galley table in Mr. Gnis's boat going across the sea to Mauritania.

In the late afternoon Hans-Peter straightened up his rooms and poured Karla down the toilet.

He had rented a minivan using a false ID, and discarded the middle seat to make room for Cari on the floor. He pulled the fuse on the inside lights in the van so he could keep the side door open in the dark.

Night was coming. Flocks of starlings settled into the hedges around Pelican Harbor Seabird Station. Two families of parrots in a bedtime dispute were louder than the music from the boats in the marina. The smell of supper on the grill and a skein of blue smoke drifted over the water.

In the parking lot beside the Seabird Station, Benito waited in his old pickup to drive Cari to the house of her cousin, where she would sleep. The A/C in the truck had not worked for years, so he had his windows down and was grateful for a breeze off the bay.

The lot was overgrown with trees and darker than the twilight.

Cari finished up in the treatment room, sterilized the instruments and took a thawed rat out to the owl.

She closed her eyes and felt the rush of wind over her as the big bird came down to seize the prize.

Benito did not want to smoke with Cari in the truck, so he rolled a cigarette in the dark to smoke now, before she came. In the dark he tapped the Bugler can with his banana fingers. He rolled the cigarette, licked it and twisted the end. He struck a kitchen match.

The match flared orange in the cab of the truck and the dart struck him in the side of the neck. He grabbed at it, the cigarette falling into his lap in a spray of sparks. He reached under the bib of his overalls for his pistol, got his hand on the pistol grip as the steering wheel swelled and wobbled in his vision and he got his hand on the handle of the door but he was hit in the neck and the dark came down fast.

Hans-Peter was conflicted as he reloaded the dart rifle. He would have loved to dissolve Benito alive in front of Cari, an orientation so to speak—WOULD THAT BE FUNNY OR WHAT?!

But time was short. He had to follow Mr. Gnis's big yacht out Government Cut to the sea and deliver Cari outside U.S. territorial waters. Better to just cut Benito's throat. Hans-Peter opened his knife. He had started across the lot to Benito's truck when the last lights went out in the Seabird Station and he heard a door shut firmly and the jingle of keys. Never mind Benito.

Cari was coming.

She was singing Shakira's part from "Mi Verdad" as she approached the truck. Benito sat behind the wheel, slumped, his chin down on his chest. Cari had a cold tamarind cola for him. Benito insisted on driving her home and often he was asleep when she came out of the station.

"Hola, mi señor."

She saw the dart in Benito's neck at the same instant she heard a crack behind her, like a palm branch breaking and felt a sting in her buttock. She reached in the truck window and got hold of Benito's gun, spun, raised the pistol, but the asphalt rose up and slammed her and the asphalt tried to wrap around her and smother her and the dark came down.

Darkness. The smell of diesel fuel and sweat and shoes. A pulse, a vibration in the metal floor, faster than a human pulse, a buzzing.

Starters whined. Two turbo diesels starting up, a rough idle, then the boat began to move. The engines settled into a low rumble, secondary vibrations going in and out of phase. *Whum whum.*

Cari opened her eyes just a little, saw the metal deck. Eyes open a little wider.

She was alone inside a cabin in the bow of a boat, lying on the floor. Above her in the center of the overhead was a clear hatch of Plexiglas, it was both a hatch and a skylight. A little light coming in the hatch and the sound changing as the boat moved out of a boathouse into the night.

A face appeared in the skylight, someone on deck looking down at her. Hans-Peter Schneider. He was wearing Antonio's earring, the Gothic cross.

Cari closed her eyes, waited a moment and opened her eyes again. A V-berth was above her as she lay on the floor. A torn and bloody fingernail, not hers, was in the seam where the footboard of the berth met the rails. Her arms and her shoulder hurt, pressed against the metal deck. Her wrists were tied behind her and her ankles bound. She could see her ankles. Four heavy-duty zip ties bound them.

She had no idea how long she had been on the boat. It was not moving very fast. She could hear the water rushing on the hull. She had been taught that the quicker after capture you escape, the better chance you have to live.

On the bridge of the long black boat with Mateo at the wheel, Hans-Peter phoned Mr. Imran aboard the two-hundred-foot yacht of Mr. Gnis, casting off for the rendezvous at sea.

"I'm on the way," Hans-Peter said. Hans-Peter could hear someone squealing near Mr. Imran.

"I'll draw a bath," Mr. Imran said.

"Good idea," Hans-Peter said. "She'll probably shit herself." The two men shared a collegial chuckle.

Down in the bow cabin Cari gingerly moved everything she could move. She did not think any bones were broken but her brow was swollen and sticky.

She warmed up her muscles, moving as well as she could, lying on her side on the deck.

Watching the skylight above her, she rolled into a sitting position, her back against the berth. It took some stretching, five tries and she was able to get her bound wrists under her buttocks and up behind her knees. She drew her knees up to her chest and with a tremendous effort got her wrists under her feet and clear. Now her hands were in front of her. She could see that the four heavy-duty zip ties on her wrists were the same type as those binding her ankles. Big ones too. The free ends stuck far out from her wrists.

The children bound in the water. The tie strips stuck far out from their wrists. They pressed the sides of their heads together. Bam!

Remembering, Cari felt a hot surge inside her and some of it was energy.

How do you get loose from tie strips? Very hard. You might break one or even two normal zip ties with leverage from a hip thrust, but not these big ones, and not four. Shim them. She could not reach the zip ties on her wrists, but she might shim the ones on her legs if she had a shim. Her cross of St. Peter with the push dagger inside was gone from her neck. She looked around the deck: any tool, a hairpin, anything.

She squirmed to see into the head, maybe there was a hairpin on the floor. Nothing. A marine toilet, a mirror, a shelf, a shower. A bathroom scale. She looked under the bunks, feeling the deck. Nothing but a smelly pair of boat shoes. What did she have that was flat and metal to use as a shim? Her push dagger was gone. Her pockets were wrong side out. She had been well frisked. She felt a scraped place on the skin of her breast, a whisker burn. Ugh. *What is flat and metal and IS THE TAB ON THE ZIPPER OF MY JEANS.*

Cari unzipped her jeans. It was slow, working the pants down her legs, working the top down over the bunched legs with her wrists tied together.

For a moment she tried to get the zipper tab into the ratchet locks on her wrists but she could not control the zipper tab without using her fingers. It just flapped back and forth. She went to work on her ankles. Two zip ties were locked in the front. She worked the tab into the ratchet lock of the top zip tie. No. No. The tongue of the ratchet kept slipping off. No. No. No. Yes. The ratchet let go, the long extra length of the zip tie sliding through the lock and it was off. She pushed the loose zip tie under a bunk so it could not be seen from above.

She rubbed the red groove in her leg and started on the next tie. It was stubborn and took twelve tries before it gave way. The next two were locked behind her legs and she had to do one of them by feel. It took ten minutes, water and distance passing under the hull. The other was loose enough to move around to the front of her leg and she got it in three tries.

But not her wrists. She could not manipulate the tab without her fingers. It just flopped against the ratchet latch.

She rested her head back against the bunk, sitting on the floor. She heard footsteps on the companionway.

She could fight with her legs free, her two hands still tied together. Hide her feet under the bunk, play possum and fake it, get a little time? No, fight now.

She got the heavy scale from the bathroom.

She got to her feet, steady steady, she raised the scale high above her head in her bound hands. The cabin door opened and she kicked Mateo in the balls so hard he was almost lifted off the floor. One more kick in the solar plexus kept him from yelling, he doubled over and she brought the scale down on the back of his head with all her strength. He went down on his face on the metal floor and she turned the scale sideways and came down on the back of his skull with the edge of it twice. The second time the thud sounded softer. The strong smell of urine came off him, a puddle spreading from under him.

There had been only a few thumps and grunts, hardly louder than the engine noise and the small impacts of the waves on the hull. Maybe Hans-Peter at the wheel had not heard. But he would definitely miss Mateo in minutes.

Hands, hands, she could not swim without hands free unless she had a float, a life jacket. None in the cabin. She frisked Mateo, hoping for a knife, a gun. Hans-Peter was too smart to send a jailer in with a weapon. Nothing useful in his pockets but some damn Chiclets.

How else can you open a zip tie? She could not swim far without her hands free. Her heaving breath brought the smells of the boat. Smells of stale sheets and old blood. Smell of urine from the dead man beside her. Foot smells of the old boat shoes with their *LEATHER LACES FRICTION SAW.*

How long did she have? Not long.

Hans-Peter yelled down the companionway. "Check her bindings and get back up here, Mateo. If you fuck her, Mateo, I will kill you. We are selling fresh meat."

Cari found the boat shoes and with her fingers and teeth took off their leather laces. She tied the laces together to make one long thong. She passed the thong over the bindings on her wrists and tied a loop in each free end.

She put her feet into the loops like stirrups and began to pump her legs in a bicycling motion, the leather thong hissing back and forth over the top zip tie on her arms as her legs pumped, smoke rising off the moving thong and the ties, heat she could feel on her arms.

Hans-Peter was yelling "Mateo, get up here you son of a bitch. I shouldn't have let you lick her tits!"

Pumping pumping, the leather thong hissing over the plastic tie. Smoke and heat and POP, the top zip tie parted, the thong stretched over the next one, hissing and smoking, POP, the second zip tie broke, and a loop slipped off her foot. It took a maddening second to get it back in place and PUMP PUMP she was driving, PUMP PUMP PUMP and POP.

PUMP PUMP PUMP PUMP PUMP PUMP POP. Her hands were free, a little numb, tingling as the blood returned to them.

She put her head up into the domed glass hatch in

time to see light passing overhead, a strip of light, lavender like the inside of a hawk's mouth, it was the underside of the causeway. Aircraft warning lights in the sky like a red star and a white one! The lights were on the tall antennas beside the Seabird Station, where her schoolbooks were, where her bag of tree fertilizer was. As the boat moved south she saw the lights of the cars on the causeway moving fast, strings of lights like tracer fire from a heavy machine gun.

Standing on the bunk she could open the skylight hatch. But the hatch was in the foredeck. Hans-Peter at the wheel would see it open. They were south of the causeway now, moving at a steady pace. She could not wait.

The engines slowed and stopped. She locked the flimsy hook on the cabin door. Hans-Peter was yelling down the companionway.

Footsteps coming down.

She pushed open the hatch and pulled herself out onto the foredeck, Hans-Peter below her kicking in the cabin door.

He had the tranquilizer rifle.

He saw the hatch was open, and he ran back up the ladder to the deck as Cari went in a clean dive off the boat and swam toward the black and fuzzy outline of Bird Key.

Hans-Peter back on deck now with the rifle, looking, looking. He swung the big spotlight on the boat, picked her up in its beam, lifted the rifle.

When the light was on her, Cari dived, finding the bottom very quickly, the water shallow enough for her to see her shadow on the sand beneath her in the spotlight beam.

She had to breathe, blow out underwater, up and gulp air, down as the flat blat of the rifle sent a dart through her hair wafting above her as she swam.

His last dart. He would have to go below for more.

Hans threw down the rifle and went back to the wheel. He could control the spotlight from the helm and the beam skipped over the water, finding Cari again. Hans-Peter gunned the boat, pursuing her. He would hit her with the fucking boat even if it killed her.

Cari could swim fast. She had never swum faster. Two big diesels churning behind her closer and closer, Bird Key closer, fifty yards.

The sound of the boat seemed to be directly over her, drawing her, the spotlight would not depress enough to keep her in its beam as the boat loomed over her. The boat struck bottom. A long crunch and scrape as it came to a stop on the sandbar off Bird Key, Hans-Peter flying into the wheel and falling to the deck. Hans-Peter up fast, on his feet.

Cari swimming, finding bottom with her hands, up and running in the water toward the black and lightless Bird Key. Running, running. Would it be better to fight him in the water? *Turn and fight him now. No, I can't kick in the water and he's got a pistol.*

Into the mangroves, onto Bird Key. Stumbling through the trash on the ground, the washed-up detritus from the pleasure boats, the flotsam from the river, broken coolers, bottles, plastic jugs, running, seeing the white objects in the dim light under the trees, stumbling over darker things, the smell of guano strong. Much muttering from the nesting birds, the sleeping flocks stirring in the trees, a loud disturbance among the ibises.

There were no clear paths, only a few overgrown trails.

It took a few moments for Hans-Peter to get his darts and drop his anchor against the rising tide, then he was in the water too, chambering a dart and wading with his long legs toward the dense mangroves at the edge of Bird Key, his pistol in his belt and his tranquilizer rifle and a flashlight in his hands.

He needed to make this pretty fast—the Marine Patrol might check his boat. It was hard going through the clumps of mangroves to reach solid ground with his hands full with his rifle and flashlight.

Cari running, stumbling, near the place where she had saved the osprey. Any weapon would do. Anything, a club, please God, a fish spear, any damn thing.

A dead bird or two on the ground, tangled in fishing line. A broken rod. An empty Miller Lite case.

Clouds sailed under a pale moon, the dim moonlight pulsing as the clouds passed under.

A thousand birds murmuring and stirring, strident peeps from some chicks until they were quieted with a snack of regurgitated fish.

A night heron worked the edges of the mangroves, stepping high, freezing with its snakelike neck cocked to strike. The night was alive.

Cari searched for a weapon on the ground until she heard Hans-Peter thrashing in the mangroves as he came ashore and then she was very quiet, pressed back into the brush, watching the pale moon shine on Hans-Peter's head. He was passing close, he had his pistol in the back of his waistband. He was wearing Antonio's earring. He would pass her in the small clearing where the osprey had hung.

She eased backward into the brush; maybe she could come up behind him and get the pistol. *Ease back, move your foot side to side to clear the ground before you put your weight on it. Don't crackle.*

A parrot flushed just above her with a loud shriek, flapping away, and Hans-Peter spun toward her, leveled the tranquilizer rifle and it cracked, the dart whizzing past her ear and he was on her, she kicking a hard one into his thigh and he was on her and she was down on her back in the brush, her hands inside against her chest. Hans-Peter was very strong, his forearm across her throat, and he was feeling in his pocket for another dart to stick in her by hand. Something touched her face, dangling from him, and she saw he was wearing her cross of St. Peter. He changed hands to find his other pocket and in the change she could butt, she butted, she butted. Her hand found the hanging cross and she snatched out the blade. It was short but not too short. She stabbed him in the soft spot behind his chin, stabbed, stabbed beneath his jaw, wagged the blade from side to side. It went up into his mouth and cut the big blood vessels under his tongue as it was made to do. He sat up choking, clutched at his face, coughed sprays of blood. She writhed from under him, he reached back for his pistol but grabbed his throat again, blew blood out his nose, and it was pumping down his chest, black in the moonlight. Heaving, bending over, away from her. Cari jerked the pistol from the back of his waistband and shot him in the spine. He slumped against the tree where the osprey had hung. He sat with his back against the tree and looked at her in the moonlight. She looked back. She looked him in the face without blinking until he died and she went to him and took back her cross.

* * *

And there they would find him in days to come, the authorities, called by some bird-watchers in a boat. They would find him sitting against the tree, buzzards on both his shoulders like the dark angels of his nature, mantling him with their black wings while they ate the soft parts of his face, his silvered canine teeth gleaming, getting the light all the time now.

Daylight was coming. The rookery stirred. Great splattings on the ground, the first flocks were up and circling, the white ibises incandescent banking across the first light. The vast roosts trembling and alive.

The light was coming up in the east. Cari could see the causeway from Bird Key, the aircraft warning lights above the Seabird Station dimming as dawn dimmed the stars. The Seabird Station, where her schoolbooks were, her bag of Vigoro, her student ID card for Miami Dade College.

Cari made some water wings with two gallon jugs, one with its cap and the other capped with a scrap of plastic bound with fishing line. Wearing her water wings, wading into the bay, not looking back, Cari swam toward the morning.

Miami Beach, Florida
2018

ACKNOWLEDGMENTS

My thanks to the Quaker United Nations Office for the field studies "The Voices of Girl Child Soldiers" by Yvonne E. Keairns, PhD.

Sergeant David Rivers (ret.), Miami-Dade Police Homicide Bureau, included me in a series of excellent homicide investigation seminars where he taught and wrote the curricula.

The Pelican Harbor Seabird Station rehabilitates injured birds and animals to resume life in the wild. It is a remarkable humane institution supported by donations and volunteers. The station welcomes visitors.

Most of all, my thanks to this place—Miami—savory and beautiful, an intensely American city built and maintained by people who came from somewhere else, often on foot.

DISCOVER THE WORLD OF HANNIBAL LECTER

A SAMPLE FROM

RED DRAGON

THOMAS HARRIS

One can only see what one observes,
and one observes only things which are
already in the mind.

ALPHONSE BERTILLON

arrow books

CHAPTER 1

Will Graham sat Crawford down at a picnic table between the house and the ocean and gave him a glass of iced tea.

Jack Crawford looked at the pleasant old house, salt-silvered wood in the clear light: 'I should have caught you in Marathon when you got off work,' he said. 'You don't want to talk about it here.'

'I don't want to talk about it anywhere, Jack. You've got to talk about it, so let's have it. Just don't get out any pictures. If you brought pictures, leave them in the briefcase – Molly and Willy will be back soon.'

'How much do you know?'

'What was in the *Miami Herald* and the *Times*,' Graham said. 'Two families killed in their houses a month apart. Birmingham and Atlanta. The circumstances were similar.'

'Not similar. The same.'

'How many confessions so far?'

'Eighty-six when I called in this afternoon,' Crawford said. 'Cranks. None of them knew details. He smashes the mirrors and uses the pieces. None of them knew that.'

'What else did you keep out of the papers?'

'He's blond, right-handed and really strong, wears a size 11 shoe. He can tie a bowline. The prints are all smooth gloves.'

'You said that in public.'

'He's not too comfortable with locks,' Crawford said. 'Used a glass-cutter and a suction-cup to get in the house last time. Oh, and his blood's AB positive.'

'Somebody hurt him?'

'Not that we know of. We typed him from semen and saliva. He's a secretor.' Crawford looked out at the flat sea. 'Will, I want to ask you something. You saw this in the papers. The second one was all over the T.V. Did you ever think about giving me a call?'

'No.'

'Why not?'

'There weren't many details at first on the one in Birmingham. It could have been anything – revenge, a relative.'

'But after the second one, you knew what it was.'

'Yeah. A psychopath. I didn't call you because I didn't want to. I know who you already have to work on this. You've got the best lab. You'd have Heimlich at Harvard, Bloom at the University of Chicago –'

'And I've got you down here fixing fucking boat motors.'

'I don't think I'd be all that useful to you, Jack. I never think about it any more.'

'Really? You caught two. The last two we had, you caught.'

'How? By doing the same things you and the rest of them are doing.'

'That's not entirely true, Will. It's the way you think.'

'I think there's been a lot of bullshit about the way I think.'

'You made some jumps you never explained.'

'The evidence was there,' Graham said.

'Sure. Sure there was. Plenty of it – afterwards. Before the collar there was so damn little we couldn't get probable cause to go in.'

'You have the people you need, Jack. I don't think I'd be an improvement. I came down here to get away from that.'

'I know it. You got hurt last time. Now you look all right.'

'I'm all right. It's not getting cut. You've been cut.'

'I've been cut, but not like that.'

'It's not getting cut. I just decided to stop. I don't think I can explain it.'

'If you couldn't look at it any more, God knows I'd understand that.'

'No. You know – having to look. It's always bad but you get so you can function anyway, as long as they're dead. The hospital, interviews, that's worse. You have to shake it off and keep on thinking. I don't believe I could do it now. I could make myself look, but I'd shut down the thinking.'

'These are all dead, Will,' Crawford said as kindly as he could.

Jack Crawford heard the rhythm and syntax of his own speech in Graham's voice. He had heard Graham do that before, with other people. Often in intense conversation Graham took on the other person's speech patterns. At first, Crawford had thought he was doing it deliberately, that it was a gimmick to get the back-and-forth rhythm going.

Later Crawford realized that Graham did it involuntarily, that sometimes he tried to stop and couldn't.

Crawford dipped into his jacket pocket with two fingers. He flipped two photographs across the table, face up.

'All dead,' he said.

Graham stared at him a moment before picking up the pictures.

They were only snapshots: a woman followed by three children and a duck carried picnic items up the bank of a pond. A family stood behind a cake.

After half a minute he put the photographs down again. He pushed them into a stack with his finger and looked far down the beach where the boy hunkered, examining something in the sand. The woman stood watching, hand on her hip, spent waves creaming around her ankles. She leaned inland to swing her wet hair off her shoulders.

Graham, ignoring his guest, watched Molly and the boy for as long as he had looked at the pictures.

Crawford was pleased. He kept the satisfaction out of his face with the same care he had used to choose the site of this conversation. He thought he had Graham. Let it cook.

Three remarkably ugly dogs wandered up and flopped to the ground around the table.

'My God,' Crawford said.

'These are probably dogs,' Graham explained. 'People dump small ones here all the time. I can give away the cute ones. The rest stay around and get to be big ones.'

'They're fat enough.'

'Molly's a sucker for strays.'

'You've got a nice life here, Will. Molly and the boy. How old is he?'

'Eleven.'

5

'Good-looking kid. He's going to be taller than you.'

Graham nodded. 'His father was. I'm lucky here. I know that.'

'I wanted to bring Phyllis down here. Florida. Get a place when I retire and stop living like a cave fish. She says all her friends are in Arlington.'

'I meant to thank her for the books she brought me in the hospital, but I never did. Tell her for me.'

'I'll tell her.'

Two small bright birds lit on the table hoping to find jelly. Crawford watched them hop around until they flew away.

'Will, this freak seems to be in phase with the moon. He killed the Jacobi family in Birmingham on Saturday night, June 28th, full moon. He killed the Leeds in Atlanta night before last, July 26th. That's one day short of a lunar month. So if we're lucky we may have a little over three weeks before he does it again.

'I don't think you want to wait here in the Keys and read about the next one in your *Miami Herald*. Hell, I'm not the Pope, I'm not saying what you ought to do, but I want to ask you, do you respect my judgement, Will?'

'Yes.'

'I think we have a better chance to get him fast if you help. Hell, Will, saddle up and help us. Go to

Atlanta and Birmingham and look, then come on to Washington. Just T.D.Y.'

Graham did not reply.

Crawford waited while five waves lapped the beach. Then he got up and slung his coat over his shoulder. 'Let's talk after dinner.'

'Stay and eat.'

Crawford shook his head. 'I'll come back later. There'll be messages at the Holiday Inn and I'll be a while on the phone. Tell Molly thanks, though.'

Crawford's rented car raised thin dust that settled on the bushes outside the shell road.

Graham returned to the table. He was afraid that this was how he would remember the end of Sugarloaf Key – ice melting in two glasses and paper napkins fluttering off the redwood table in the breeze and Molly and Willy far down the beach.

Sunset on Sugarloaf, the herons still and the red sun swelling.

Will Graham and Molly Foster Graham sat on a bleached drift log, their faces orange in the sunset, backs in violet shadow. She picked up his hand.

'Crawford stopped by to see me at the shop before he came out here,' she said. 'He asked directions to the house. I tried to call you. You really ought to answer the phone once in a while. We saw the car when we got home and went round to the beach.'

'What else did he ask you?'

'How you are.'

'And you said?'

'I said you're fine and he should leave you the hell alone. What does he want you to do?'

'Look at evidence. I'm a forensic specialist, Molly. You've seen my diploma.'

'You mended a crack in the ceiling paper with your diploma, I saw that.' She straddled the log to face him. 'If you missed your other life, what you used to do, I think you'd talk about it. You never do. You're open and calm and easy now … I love that.'

'We have a good time, don't we?'

Her single styptic blink told him he should have said something better. Before he could fix it, she went on.

'What you did for Crawford was bad for you. He has a lot of other people – the whole damn government I guess – why can't he leave us alone?'

'Didn't Crawford tell you that? He was my supervisor the two times I left the F.B.I. Academy to go back to the field. Those two cases were the only ones like this he ever had, and Jack's been working a long time. Now he's got a new one. This kind of psychopath is very rare. He knows I've had … experience.'

'Yes, you have,' Molly said. His shirt was unbuttoned and she could see the looping scar across his stomach.

It was finger-width and raised and it never tanned. It ran down from his left hip-bone and turned up to notch his rib-cage on the other side.

Dr. Hannibal Lecter did that with a linoleum knife. It happened a year before Molly met Graham and it very nearly killed him. Dr. Lecter, known in the tabloids as 'Hannibal the Cannibal', was the second psychopath Graham had caught.

When he finally got out of hospital, Graham resigned from the Federal Bureau of Investigation, left Washington, and found a job as a diesel mechanic in the boat-yard at Marathon in the Florida Keys. It was a trade he grew up with. He slept in a trailer at the boat-yard until Molly and her good ramshackle house on Sugarloaf Key.

Now he straddled the drift log and held both her hands. Her feet burrowed under his.

'All right, Molly. Crawford thinks I have a knack for the monsters. It's like a superstition with him.'

'Do you believe it?'

Graham watched three pelicans fly in line across the tidal flats. 'Molly, an intelligent psychopath – particularly a sadist – is hard to catch for several reasons. First, there's no traceable motive. So you can't go that way. And most of the time you won't have any help from informants. See, there's a lot more stooling than sleuthing behind most arrests, but in a case like this there won't *be* any informants. *He* may not even know that he's doing it. So you have to take whatever evidence you have and extrapolate. You try to reconstruct his thinking. You try to find patterns.'

'And follow him and find him,' Molly said. 'I'm afraid if you go after this maniac, or whatever he is – I'm afraid he'll do you like the last one did. That's it. That's what scares me.'

'He'll never see me or know my name, Molly. The police, they'll have to take him down if they can find him, not me. Crawford just wants another point of view.'

She watched the red sun spread over the sea. High cirrus glowed above it.

Graham loved the way she turned her head, artlessly giving him her less perfect profile. He could see the pulse in her throat, and remembered suddenly and completely the taste of salt on her skin. He swallowed and said, 'What the hell can I do?'

'What you've already decided. If you stay here and there's more killing, maybe it would sour this place for you. *High Noon* and all that crap. If it's that way, you weren't really asking.'

'If I *were* asking, what would you say?'

'Stay here with me. Me. Me. Me. And Willy, I'd drag him in if it would do any good. I'm supposed to dry my eyes and wave my hanky. If things don't go so well, I'll have the satisfaction that you did the right thing. That'll last about as long as Taps. Then I can go home and switch one side of the blanket on.'

'I'd be at the back of the pack.'

'Never in your life. I'm selfish, huh?'

'I don't care.'

'Neither do I. It's keen and sweet here. All the things that happened to you before make you know it. Value it, I mean.'

He nodded.

'Don't want to lose it either way,' she said.

'Nope. We won't either.'

Darkness fell quickly and Jupiter appeared, low in the southwest.

They walked back to the house beside the rising gibbous moon. Far out past the tidal flats, bait fish leaped for their lives.

Crawford came back after dinner. He had taken off his coat and tie and rolled up his sleeves for the casual effect. Molly thought Crawford's thick pale forearms were repulsive. To her he looked like a damnably wise ape. She served him coffee under the porch fan and sat with him while Graham and Willy went out to feed dogs. She said nothing. Moths batted softly at the screens.

'He looks good, Molly,' Crawford said. 'You both do – skinny and brown.'

'Whatever I say, you'll take him anyway, won't you?'

'Yeah. I have to. I have to do it. But I swear to God, Molly, I'll make it as easy on him as I can. He's changed. It's great you got married.'

'He's better and better. He doesn't dream so often now. He was really obsessed with the dogs for a while. Now he just takes care of them; he doesn't talk about them all the time. You're his friend, Jack. Why can't you leave him alone?'

'Because it's his bad luck to be the best. Because he doesn't think like other people. Somehow he never got in a rut.'

'He thinks you want him to look at evidence.'

'I do want him to look at evidence. There's nobody better with evidence. But he has the other thing too. Imagination, projection, whatever. He doesn't like that part of it.'

'You wouldn't like it either if you had it. Promise me something, Jack. Promise me you'll see to it he doesn't get too close. I think it would kill him to have to fight.'

'He won't have to fight. I can promise you that.'

When Graham finished with the dogs, Molly helped him pack.

RED DRAGON

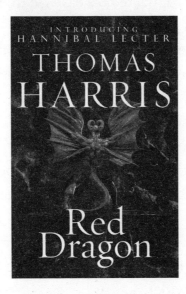

'The best popular novel since *The Godfather*.'
Stephen King

The novel that launched Hannibal Lecter's legacy
of evil.

Sexual hunger; demonic violence; sinister logic –
the lethal components of a deadly formula driving a
psychopath in the grip of an unimaginable delusion;
a boastful killer who sends the police tormenting notes;
a tortured, torturing monster who finds ultimate
pleasure in viciously murdering happy families, and
calls himself… The Red Dragon.

THE SILENCE OF THE LAMBS

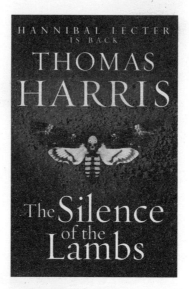

'Thrillers don't come any better than this.' Clive Barker

THE LEGENDARY PSYCHOLOGICAL THRILLER

An FBI trainee. A psychopath locked up for unspeakable crimes. And a serial killer getting ever closer to his latest victim...

FBI rookie Clarice Starling turns to Dr. Hannibal Lecter, monster cannibal held in a hospital for the criminally insane, for insight into the deadliest madman she must find. As Dr. Lecter invites her into the darkest chambers of his mind, he forces her to confront her own childhood demons as the price of understanding, an unspeakable tuition he exacts to teach her how the monster thinks. And time is running out...

HANNIBAL

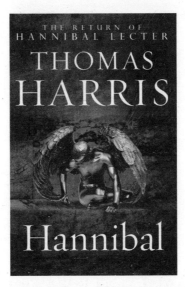

'A gut-churning, nail-biting, skin-crawling triumph –
addictive on every level.' *Express*

Seven years have passed since Dr. Hannibal Lecter
escaped from custody, seven years since FBI Special
Agent Clarice Starling interviewed him in a max-
imum security hospital for the criminally insane.
The doctor is still at large, but Starling has never
forgotten her encounters with Dr. Lecter, and the
metallic rasp of his seldom-used voice still sounds
in her dreams...

HANNIBAL RISING

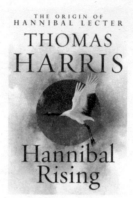

THE ORIGIN OF
HANNIBAL LECTER
THOMAS
HARRIS

Hannibal
Rising

'Prepare to be thrillingly nauseated.' *Sunday Times*

HANNIBAL LECTER WASN'T BORN A MONSTER. HE WAS MADE ONE.

Hannibal Lecter emerges from the nightmare of the Eastern Front, a boy in the snow, mute, with a chain around his neck. He seems utterly alone, but he has brought his demons with him.

Hannibal's uncle, a noted painter, finds him in a Soviet orphanage and brings him to France, where Hannibal will live with his uncle and his uncle's beautiful and exotic wife, Lady Murasaki.

Lady Murasaki helps Hannibal to heal, and he flourishes, becoming the youngest person ever admitted to medical school in France. But Hannibal's demons visit him and torment him. When he is old enough, he visits them in turn. He discovers that he has gifts beyond the academic, and in that epiphany, Hannibal Lecter becomes death's prodigy.